OBOE WOES

a novel

Donald L. Simons

Oboe Woes, a novel
By Donald L. Simons

Crescendo Publishing, LLC
2-558 Upper Gage Ave., Ste. 246
Hamilton, ON L8V 4J6
Canada

GetPublished@CrescendoPublishing.com
1-877-575-8814

ISBN: 978-1-948719-08-7 (p)
ISBN: 978-1-948719-09-4 (e)

Printed in the United States of America
Cover design by AleMiglio
10 9 8 7 6 5 4 3 2 1

Table of Contents

Chapter One
Alternative Oboing

*A*n oboist with dramatic tendencies was how Hieronymus Hup, the conductor of the Stiff Arm Symphony described N. Emopee, his Third Oboist, third out of three, for the past three years, the same position N. Emopee held previously, and for the same number of years, with the Embouchure Ensemble over in Westhill. Prior to that he was a plumber. Tendencies or not, he was not without accomplishment, able, for instance, to play from memory every piece of oboe music ever written, including Handel, Hayden, Mozart, Beethoven, Schumann, Nielsen, and Britten, and all in one sitting. His problem now, though, was his eyesight, a distance vision no longer with any distance to it. Even with contact lenses and glasses together, it had become so poor that he could no longer see the conductor, couldn't make out old Hup up there. As a consequence Hup had to let him go. It was one thing to march to the beat of a different drummer and quite another to oboe to the beat of a different conductor. N. Emopee's only option was to get into a different line of work, where he'd be closer in.

And so here he stood in the front window of the lobby of Popcorn Pictures where he watched the Geo Metros flipping past like film across the lens of a camera. Even here in the mountains it was all pace; time was money. His jittery hand dropped again into the manila envelope at his side, not that he didn't know what his resume contained already; he could recite it word for word. Rather was it for his confidence, which needed a boost just then.

His confidence needed a boost? He was N. Emopee, Third-Oboist. His gray cape got a toss, and he fingered his fawn fedora. Overhead, all the while, a four-bladed ceiling fan whirled, flap, flap, at which he swatted like at a fly, until, finally, he escaped it by plopping onto a far-off sofa. A cream-white leather job it was, with lavender cushions no less. Someone's stubbed-out cigarette, not all the way out yet, gasped its last in a Coke can on the adjacent table. Coke smoke, a choke from N. Emopee.

Popcorn Pictures lay on a bustling boulevard in Hollywoods, West Virginia, the California Hollywood, the one without the "s" on the end, having collapsed five years earlier, no longer able to afford itself. This Hollywoods, aka "the Woods," appropriate to West Virginia, the new lean-

and-mean, low-overhead transplanted California Hollywood, began at Route 119, now Ritchie Bordeaux Way. It was named for the famous local comedian who made it in the big time. First he was the sidekick to Andy Griffin on television, and then a fish in a movie. Freshly planted down the middle with white- and pink-flowering dogwood trees, a far cry from the lemon trees of the western Hollywood, "RB Way" nonetheless made an impressive main street for Hollywoods.

This was N. Emopee's second interview of the day, his first an hour earlier over in the Haines building, named for Senator Stagner Haines whose political "pork" was responsible for much of this relocation of Hollywood to Hollywoods. That meeting, though, was not really an interview so much as a what, a "get acquainted session" the man called it. As with Popcorn Pictures, Famous Films was not advertising a-different-line-of-work-for-unemployed-Third-Chair-oboists either, although admittedly not really an issue here in the biz where one put himself out there and if he had more to offer than the person presently in the post a switch was made.

Clearly, though, the producer there at Famous Films was secure enough in his job. He looked the stereotypical showbiz mogul, fifty years old, receding dyed-white hair, a loose linen sport shirt, dyed pink, open at the collar to reveal his dyed tan. And, oh yes, a big bling gold neck chain.

N. Emopee, for his part, was wearing his deep blue silk suit, the one he wore in China, dared to wear only in Asia, where, unlike here in the States, there were no silkworm-rights activists. That he was willing to risk it on this occasion was because the West Virginia silkworm-rights activists were all out of town, were up at a sit-in in Punxsutawney, Pennsylvania, with the groundhog-rights activists. A solidarity thing. And, yes, finally, a five-alarm red tie, made of silk too, that hung dramatically at his lungs, to where at thirty-three years old he looked thirty-two again.

Was it this tie that shifted the producer's conversation from filming oboe concerts for cable television, to sex? Finally, though, the question "You're not married, are you?" exposed the real reason N. Emopee had been invited here; "it might be something or it might be nothing," the producer had said to him cryptically over the phone.

"Married?" N. Emopee, his flat face even flatter.

Then again the discussion switched back and forth.

"It would be great if you, with your knowledge of oboe music, could let me see scores with lots of sex in them." The man was gesticulating testicularly.

N. Emopee blinked once, then twice. "But will it get me a job here?"

"Well, you think about it," the producer, once more at N. Emopee's long red tie with a sigh.

Flattered, embarrassed, N. Emopee smiled, frankly, and left it at that. And then left. But not before the producer remarked, unexpectedly, at the door, "Haven't I seen you before?" an odd thing for him to say.

Here at Popcorn Pictures, though, things looked more to the matter. He had at least heard of Popcorn, had seen somewhere the name of producer-director Calvin Crump, a legend in the biz. As it happened, it was the only name N. Emopee recognized in his source for this job search.

Then, there was good reason for his not knowing anyone else in this business. He was an oboist, and in this instance an oboist attempting to cross over into either television or film, remembering that he had worked up in Pittsburgh for a time, for the Remarkable Broadcasting Corporation, RBC, television and film, albeit as a stagehand and then a plumber. What this "cross over into" would be exactly, and how it would work out, he wasn't quite sure. He'd have to wait and see, see how it shook out. Just so it was in the biz. He was set on working in the biz.

His resume back into its envelope he eyed the receptionist's desk where a local farm boy, by the look of him, with a Ronald Coleman mustache, was studying what appeared to be a page-long list of appointments, and whose bloodshot eyes evidenced that he had been working there all night. Into the lobby, though, they now abruptly darted, where they found a chalk-faced girl with hair and heels to match.

"Me?" she bleated.

To her feet, her Kmart cologne, Raspberry something, wafting into the air, she quickly tiptoed clickety-click the whole way down the hall, whereupon like a tissue dispenser another girl of identical description was soon in her place. That these were actresses auditioning for the same role N. Emopee had no doubt, Popcorn Pictures noted, or notorious, depending on one's level of appreciation, for their horror movies and sci-fi thrillers. Still, it bothered him that these performers looked so led-to-the-slaughter, stressed-out-led-to-the-slaughter, just like the guy at the desk.

Then, Popcorn hired people right out of the local college, he had read, new graduates keen and not asking many questions. "This would have to be the case," N. Emopee, under his breath, Popcorn also famous, or infamous, depending on one's depth of research, for their tight purse strings, even when they were back on the west coast. The real attraction of such companies was that many now big wigs in the biz, directors like Coppola, and movie stars like Nicholson, started their careers with them, why, in fact, N. Emopee was here.

"Mr. Emopee?"

N. Emopee, wide eyed now, clambered to his fallen arches. This voice, however, in all its firmness, was not that of the farm boy at the front desk, but of Mabelondra, or so she said her name was, a six-foot-three secretary, muscular to her toes, a fitness type obviously, whom N. Emopee found pacing beside his chair. But now wasn't that her in the ad poster on the wall for "Space Shenanigans," her obviously the shenanigans? His cape back to reveal its oboic orange lining, he and Mabelondra then marched lockstep around the corner and into the private office of the boss.

"Mr. Crump will be with you momentarily," Mabelondra to N. Emopee as she turned. "Can I get you anything?"

"How about a job?" N. Emopee, smiling. No sooner had this hit his lips, though, and just as the shag couch in the center of the room met his bottom, he was on his feet again, this time shaking the wrist of Mr. Crump; Mr. Crump had no right hand, one handshake too many it appeared.

"How do you do?" the producer, a crisp articulation like someone who had done voice-overs all his life. "Please sit down."

N. Emopee looked where he had just been, then lowered once again, or for the first time truly, onto the thick black shag couch, like onto the back of a yak, anxious bubbles to his anxious brow. He then watched as Crump gained his vast desk just beside the room's bay window, where Crump went on to say, "Excuse me for a moment, won't you?"

N. Emopee nodded once, then grinned bravely.

This Crump, now that N. Emopee had a minute to survey him, looked as though he'd just stepped from a Jacuzzi, face all flush, or was it drugs? Whatever it was, Crump was all business now, the receiver of his phone between his ear and shoulder, as if it grew there.

So, this was the legendary Calvin "Cal" Crump, "King of 'B' Movies," the guy who specialized, according to flick critic Lex Rexroth in the Movie Times, in low-budget films, the revenues from which sustained him while he pursued the occasional more serious feature, which he hoped ultimately would be his legacy; he had had some good reviews. "Asteroid Noises" had some good notices. Still he looked shot, didn't they all look shot here at Popcorn, worried, harried, and spent? Was this what N. Emopee had to look forward to, too, were he hired?

Just then Crump dumped the receiver of his phone back onto its stand, a large pink pad getting a scratch from his left-handed pen. Staring thoughtfully, Barrymorely, out the bay window, to which he had just swiveled, he was recalling the best moments of his life, to see him, or was it the best movies of his career, the same thing, most likely, "Mad Buttons," most likely, or was he wondering where his next line of cocaine would be coming from?

A minute later, however, his gray eyes, with the sixty years of baggage under them, were from his window back around to N. Emopee, who, to kill the seeming eternity, was contemplating the rug in front of him, an oriental affair with a mystical mandala in the middle of it, or so it appeared to him to be, if it wasn't the logo of Japan Airways.

"So then, N., may I call you N.? Thank you for your letter."

N. Emopee went to speak.

"But you see our employment needs at present--"

"I have a resume with me if you'd like to see it, hot off the press, as they say, pressed to a tee." N. Emopee hauled out, then held out the sheet.

"Actually, I believe I have a copy of it here in front of me, thank you," an awkward pause while Crump's eyes filmed the page. "As I was about to say," he continued, "we have all the oboists we need at present--"

"Well, it's not really oboing I'm looking for, to be honest with you--"

"--although I anticipate an assistant producer's position in another month, a post I'm willing to consider you for, if you are at all interested."

"An assistant producer's position?" N. Emopee was taken aback, higher up the feeding chain than he expected so soon.

"Reading scripts, inspecting locations, making deals with contractors, and, oh, yes, answering telephones, we all answer phones around here."

"Of course, you do."

"I don't know what your current situation is," the producer, his pen again to his only hand, "but if you need something right away, something to tide you over, I can put you to work unloading trucks."

The smile drained from N. Emopee's face. The fact was, he had had his share of unloading trucks the last time out, as a stagehand at Remarkable Broadcasting Corporation in Pittsburgh, which had left him, before it was over, feeling like a long-haul mover.

"By the way I see here that you worked in Pittsburgh. What was an oboist doing in Pittsburgh?"

N. Emopee blinked.

"I mean how did you happen to go up there?"

Since his return to West Virginia via a gubernatorial pardon, N. Emopee had given a stock explanation to this, to people he didn't know, that is, to those whose politics he didn't know, and so it was here again that he said, simply, "a job opportunity I couldn't pass up," even though it didn't sound convincing. Still, he wasn't about to reveal his opposition to the latest Hayfields and McCays war there in West Virginia, not to a guy who might be a brigadier general for all he knew, look at Jimmy Stewart.

"I'll have to think about the unloading trucks part," N. Emopee, a breath at last. "As for the assistant producer's job, well, I am interested, completely interested. I particularly like to read scripts. I took a drama class one time, you see."

"You don't say."

"We read a lot of scripts. Plays, naturally."

"Naturally. Whose plays did you read?"

"Are you familiar with Michel de Ghelderode, by chance?"

Crump's face leveled, but not without a wink. "You might refresh my memory. "

"Then he's scarcely known in America, no reason for you to have heard of him, an academic thing. But, you know, it's material you'd love, I'll bet, sentimental executioners, deranged monks, mystical clowns--"

Crump brightened.

"I mean if you like spectacle. I wrote a whole paper on it."

"You'd be willing to show me this paper, would you?"

As with Famous Films, here again N. Emopee could see the biz preying on the naïve, out to get something for nothing, standard practice here it looked like. Still, "I'd like to sleep on it, if you don't mind, sir. I'll get back to you the first thing tomorrow morning."

"Sure, N.," Crump. But not before Crump added, "Haven't I seen you before?"

There it was again. What was up with that?

N. Emopee lived thirty-minutes away, in Morganhill, in a big house on Pound Down Street, less a street than a drive, and less a drive than a lane, with Circle Road how one got there. One Pound Down Street was the only residence on the street, lane, which was to say there was no Two Pound Down Street, even though there was enough land for a Two--and a Three, and a Four Pound Down Streets, and quite large Two, Three, and Fours, except that back in the day, N. Emopee's father, Rem, bought up the whole hill.

Accordingly, One Pound Down Street was at the very top of this hill, a spot which was got to round and round, barber pole fashion, from bottom to top, at the very peak of which was a circle, hence Circle Road, which encircled all of One Pound Down Street. Rem objected to the name Circle Road, as if he lived in a bull's eye, preferring a more appropriate designation. The new name should cover the entire route, including Circle Road, except that the city council objected to it. They said that the current street signs did not have enough room for the additional letters that, say, Barber Pole Boulevard would require, and they sure as heck were not going to pay to put all new street signs up there, even though there was only one of them, just to please Rem Emopee.

Besides, no one else, no one other than the Emopees, ever went up that way, save for the odd painter sprucing things up at the house.

That evening, N. Emopee paced from one end of the house to the other, or rather from one end of his small apartment in the back of the house to the other, from the sliding glass doors of the pine-paneled lanai, to the plaid living room, to the hall with the steel sculpture of a phoenix, to the study with the historic oboes in a case, back to the hall with the steel sculpture, and into his bedroom in midnight blue, only to wind up again at the kitchen table, where he launched into a typical soliloquy:

"The answer is simple enough," he had to admit to himself; "I don't want to work in 'schlock,' in 'B' movies. Why didn't I realize that before I went all the way over to Popcorn? I could have saved myself, to say nothing of Crump, a lot of trouble. Sure, I want to get back into television and film, but in the <u>majors</u>. My worry is, if I start out in schlock, I'll be in schlock the rest of my life. I'll be schlockified."

He stopped. "But now am I being too picky, maybe, too particular? At the same time, I want to feel satisfied in the job? Why should I work at something such as unloading trucks, or at a fried assistant producer's position that I'd surely be miserable doing and would probably bale out of after a week's time, when I could be hired in the majors instead?"

It was dark now on the grounds around the house, except for the security light light-up just then when an opossum tipped over the trash barrel. The opossum, though, was joined this time by N. Emopee himself, standing there gazing up at his residence in what could only be termed a quandary. His whiskered face bunched up like paper mache, he, to his own amazement even, was pondering selling the place. It would be to pay off the loan he took out against it the previous year, which was to pay off a loan of his father's for the house, too. Foreclosure was next.

Yet, how realistic was this parting of his with the house, remembering that his father, Rem, had COMMANDED him, frankly, to one day convert it to a home for the RFW, Remnants of Foreign Wars. "Swear," Rem to him as though N. Emopee's life depended on it.

Rem, after all, had come from a foreign war, from the Battle of Cape Emopee on the Island of Emopee in the Red Sea, the United States having gone to war with the tiny island for twenty minutes one time, on a Thursday, to do with docking privileges.

Rem and his wife Florence had been conscripts into the Island of Emopee Army, the IEA, but sadly Florence died in the war, leaving poor Rem and his eight-year old son N. Emopee, whom it so happened was drafted into the army as well to hold his mother's purse, all on their own. This was in 1902.

But now Rem and N. Emopee, following a two-year stint in a U. S. remnants-of-war camp in the desert somewhere, stowed away in the hold of a sorghum ship bound for Philadelphia. They were on their way to a new life, they hoped, hopefully in New Zealand. Once States-side, they hitchhiked west, naturally, only to come down with pneumonia, both of them, in West Virginia. There they were taken in by Compassionate Cottage there in Morganhill, a home for sick remnants of foreign wars on their way to New Zealand. Morganhill, however, with its hills and valley, was so like their hometown back on the Island of Emopee, they decided to stay.

As an adult, after earning a fortune as an entrepreneur, his company Running Shoes by Rem was a runaway success, even in 1902, or to be exact, in 1908, Rem vowed to make his own house the same kind of sanctuary as Compassionate Cottage, only bigger and better. Thus began what became the big house on the hill, always with the purpose of converting it, eventually, to a haven for foreign war remnants.

"I can't in good conscience sell the place now, can I?" N. Emopee.

"Back for more, eh?" This was Jon Doh, an anonymous Korean-American, who was helping N. Emopee find prospective employers in the biz. This was at the American Film Institute's Portis Library there in Hollywoods. Caleb Portis was a renowned local actor, famous for his portrayal of Yorick's skull in Don Mealy's production of Shakespeare's Hamlet, or Hamlet Come Home, as Mealy titled it. The library was on Wharf Street at Decker's Creek, at the beginning of Ritchie Bordeaux Way. Doh, as he was called, was a research librarian there.

"Determination by any other name," N. Emopee, as he shook the shaky hand of the stocky Doh. Despite a pleasant non-threatening, non-defensive demeanor, which included a disarmingly broad smile, Doh had an unexpected jitteriness about him that had N. Emopee on edge too. Why didn't Doh calm down? After all, it wasn't as though they didn't know each other. Doh's nervousness might be, or so N. Emopee speculated, the result of his, N. Emopee's, revealing that he was a third oboist, the former Third Oboist with the Stiff Arm Symphony in Morganhill, and, prior to this, Third Oboist with the not quite so well-known Embouchure Ensemble across the river in Westhill. This was interpreted by the librarian to mean, possibly, that he, Doh, had better be on his toes, not at all why N. Emopee had mentioned it to him. Simply, he wanted Doh to take him seriously in this search of his for a job in the biz.

But then why would Doh not take him at his word? It was just that N. Emopee figured that the librarian had seen scores of the starry-eyed over his time at AFI. When would come his wink to the other staffers there that here was another one, another dreamer?

"So, how did the interviews go for you at Popcorn and Famous?" Doh being the one who had directed N. Emopee to the *Blue Book of Film and Television Production Companies*, the source of the first five companies N. Emopee had written to, with resume, including Popcorn and Famous.

N. Emopee, backing back from the librarian, frowned once, his eyes quickly finding the high plaster ceiling and then the line of tense oak tables in the middle of the room. Streaming, all the while, through the poplar trees at the far bank of windows, the Hollywoods sun lit up the wicker periodicals stand which held *The Hollywoods Reporter* and *Daily Vanity* trade papers.

"Famous wasn't anything," N. Emopee to Doh, finally; "the guy was only interested in my tie, if you know what I mean."

Doh stared.

"As for Popcorn, everybody there looked bushed, pounded to a pulp, heaved to a heap."

"Heavens."

"Wasted to a wisp."

"Sorry to hear it."

"Never mind that it's schlock."

"Pardon me?"

"Popcorn is Schlock, second class citizenship in the biz. And I'll tell you, too, that I'm feeling rather put off by it all just now."

"Yet, here you are, again."

"Here I am again, indeed," N. Emopee with a sigh.

"It's the lure of the biz," Doh, sagely, "the biz, the answer to everything."

"Mara the Tempter?"

Another blank from Doh.

"Buddhism." N. Emopee thought a Korean anything would know of Buddhism's Satan, thought that because the monk Sundo had taken Buddhism to Korea in the Fourth Century, that Doh would have heard of him by now, not to stereotype Doh.

"Oh," the best Doh could offer. "But like I told you last week," the librarian forging ahead, "work of any kind in the biz is hard to come by in the best of times, doubly so now, in that the industry is off by fifty percent. Studios and production companies are down-sizing, since their move here to West Virginia."

N. Emopee tightened.

Now at the corner door leading to the stacks in back, Doh turned around, adding, "The difference is that you have unique qualifications, the Stiff Arm Symphony for one, which sets you apart from the pack. My hunch is that the right biz company will snap you up in an instant."

"Really?"

"Just remember that even if you do get hired, the chances are it will be on the lowest rung. In this town everyone works his way up from the bottom, even Stiff Arm Third Oboists."

Was this a slam? As one in the biz already, even if only marginally, Doh was entitled to it. But, still, there was the nagging impression that Doh was not taking him seriously, that Doh saw something in him that N. Emopee did not see in himself, and that it was not a guy in the biz.

Chapter Two
Looking for Luck

*L*eaving One Pound Down Street the next morning, N. Emopee felt all the worse for the oppressive heat of the day, from the Fairfield winds, so-called, hot enough to melt the soles off his old Burgattis. The Fairfield winds? Fairfield used to be a town twenty miles south of Morganhill, down river, except that a production company over in the Woods bought it out and turned it into a desert. This was for a remake of *Lawrence of Arabia*, to be called *Lawrence of Fairfield*. Now every summer the southerly winds came across that desert and up the river, making everyone in Morganhill miserable.

At the office complex, were ten offices a complex? where N. Emopee had a small space, the metal flap to his mailbox, in the complex of flaps, got a lift, where he discovered a letter from, of all people, CineProd. This was a production company he interviewed with a month earlier, and who promised to get back to him after they talked it over. Was this his lucky break?

The man he had spoken with at Cineprod was a past vice president of creative affairs at Universal Artists, while his boss, the owner of CineProd, who had interviewed him as well, before the day was done, had been a vice president in charge of programming at CBA-TV, a senior vice president in charge of production at GMG studios, and a president and chief executive officer at Colorful Pictures. Depending upon what was on the other side of this envelope, these might well be his new bosses, something he'd better get used to. In fact, he might have a title of his own, now, too, N. Emopee CEO, Chief Executive Oboist.

But alas,

Dear Mr. Emopee: The last time we spoke I had in mind the creation of a Director of Development position, for which it appeared you were well enough qualified. Principally, I was looking to free myself of time in the office, enabling me to be out onsite more often. However, today the company president has informed me that Development position could not be established until at least late October, by which time I am certain you will have found appropriate employment elsewhere. Good luck in your search.

Sincerely yours, Tru Bucks, and Mo Gul

But, now, N. Emopee wondered why it was that everyone in the Woods was either twenty-five or fifty years old, and how someone in his mid-twenties, such as this Tru Bucks, who had the first shot at him, could already have been vice president of creative affairs at Universal Artists, or vice president of anything for that matter? Even the fifty-year-old Mo Gul, how could he have had <u>that</u> many bizly jobs in his career? He must have been at each for seven minutes.

His faded, sweating face to his building's rear stairwell, N. Emopee climbed to the second floor, where he inserted his nameless key into his titleless door, or almost titleless door, for still on it was "N. Emopee, Third Oboist," even though he no longer had that job.

The thanks-but-no-thanks letter onto his desk, he would have had the corners of his mouth all the way down were he not <u>nearly</u> the Director of Development at CineProd, just that close. With a poke of the pink button, the cool-hi button, on his faithful Airwaves air conditioner, there came a bone-rattling roar, followed by a blandly refrigerated blast, in front of which he sat for as long as it lasted.

So he wanted to be a director of development, or whatever it might be, did he, a substantial job in the biz? But did he want what went with it? Two weeks at it and his nerves would be frayed, like all the others he'd seen around Hollywoods, frayed and shot? What did he think he was doing anyway? He should be glad CineProd was not hiring him.

At his far filing cabinet, he removed a binder, black in color not surprisingly, a place for him to file the eighteen rejection letters from the university presses not interested in his drama class term paper, "Michel de Ghelderode: Sentimental Executioners, Deranged monks, and Mystical clowns," but in which now, in the next available clear polypropylene top-loading sheet protector, he added his latest thumbs down, this time from CineProd.

For someone with so much to offer, it was amazing how no one as yet had, as Doh put it, snapped him up. All the individuals, academic and in Hollywoods, to whom he'd written had not even bothered to send him a rejection letter. He wasn't even worth the price of a stamp.

Why he should think of it just then he could not say, a feeling of futility maybe, but it occurred to him suddenly why not teach? "Why not teach?" he said to himself out loud. His dad, Rem, after all, was a teacher at one point.

Prior to his long-running running shoe business, and long before he taught a course at the local community college, N. Emopee's father Rem had ideas for other businesses on his drawing board. N. Emopee came upon them one day. These ideas included: a stool with two legs for three-cornered rooms; a bus that would only run if there are six people in it; a dog food that when pooped evaporated; powdered shovels; a car with a five-cylinder engine that ran on four cylinders, but with a spare; a one-legged cow that consisted of an udder with a leg under it. The latter was inspired by Salvador

Dali quite obviously, for whom Rem had a considerable appreciation. At the bottom of the list was "running shoes that run themselves," that resulted in Rem's business. He even retained "running shoes that run themselves" as his ad slogan.

Professors Roger Blodgett and Joe Bag were N. Emopee's advisors when he attended the University of Southern California, USC, in Los Angeles, to learn the oboe. USC had since relocated to West Virginia, too, for the same reason as the biz. They subsequently changed their name to USC in the Woods. Meeting with them again would, ostensibly, be to ask them how they had been, but then, "I'm thinking of teaching," he would announce. If they were not immediately enthusiastic about it, he would drop the whole thing at once. If, on the other hand, they liked the idea, all bets were off. They might even make vacancies in their own departments available to him.

As his plan was to poke his head in Blodgett's door for only a minute, at first anyway, he was surprised when it was noon before Blodgett even turned up, and then it was just to lock his door on his way to the campus restaurant. When it occurred to Blodgett that N. Emopee did after all have an appointment, he suggested that the two of them have lunch together. N. Emopee had just downed a sandwich from the hall vending machine moments earlier, but "Sounds good," he burped.

As they settled at their table in the restaurant, N. Emopee struggled with how to make his declaration. Blodgett, by contrast, was content just to shoot the breeze, not wishing to engage in shop talk, so to say, if this was what N. Emopee intended. "How's the soup?" to him instead.

Put simply, Blodgett sensed that his former student was merely being desperate, something to do with a job search no doubt, a matter which would resolve itself soon enough, no need for him to get involved. Indeed, didn't he disappear midway through their meal, visiting with his colleagues at other tables around the room? And then, finally, when he did come back and it came time for them to depart, confusion broke out over who should pay the tab. N. Emopee planned on business, Blodgett only a hello. As it happened, N. Emopee never did get to his subject, teaching. Were he more convinced of it himself, he would have been more insistent.

His meeting with Professor Bag, though, was more helpful. Bag, in fact, after N. Emopee finally brought up the matter of teaching, led the way. He talked about the upcoming A.O.A., American Oboe Association, convention in St. Louis, allowing that it was especially useful for job seekers. He went on to reveal that he himself was going to attend, to deliver a speech on the future of the oboing profession. N. Emopee, he said, should go. "However, it's a case of two hundred people after twenty positions," Bag, quite honestly, "and, from your standpoint, only two of those jobs might be what you are looking for exactly. But the competition is so intense that if you have no teaching experience, which you don't, or are not believable as a teacher, which you aren't, the odds are against you from the get-go."

N. Emopee swallowed once, then beamed crookedly.

"Your best bet," Bag, his long index finger pointing skyward, as if to burst a balloon, N. Emopee's balloon, "is to go for a technical job, of which there are always an abundance."

N. Emopee cringed. "Technical, eh? Repairing?"

The parking structure beside the new student union building was where N. Emopee had left his car, the climb back across campus a reminder of the heat. Still blowing were the Fairfield winds, the hot breezes from over at the Fairfield desert, so that his tousled hair was once again tossing. At 5:00 p.m. it remained 100 degrees outside. A low stone bench beneath a high willow tree at the entrance of the student union served him as a brief oasis.

His vastly dissimilar meetings of the day, as he reflected on them there on the bench, astonished even him, exchanges during which, by the end of them, had both professors more interested in his Hollywoods aspirations than in his plans regarding teaching. Blodgett, in fact, on their walk back to his office, said, "They tell me you need to know somebody to get into that business," with Bag suggesting, "You could get a part-time technical position at one of the local trade colleges while you continue your try for the biz."

What was he to make of this? Pulling to his feet, he stepped to the great marble fountain, Ruby Blades Fountain, gurgling noisily just in front of him, a willow twig, his fiddlestick of the past ten minutes flopping into the waiting surge. What he made of it was that Hollywoods was okay, that there was no reason why he should feel guilty about his biz ambitions, that just because he was trained to play the oboe was no reason why he had to teach it. Indeed, as the professors implied, he was lucky to have the option of doing something different. They didn't.

Just then the pay phone next to him rang sharply. N. Emopee lifted the receiver, only to find Professor Bag on the other end. "You left your pen here, N." N. Emopee had heard of omniscient professors, but this was ridiculous.

Hick's Used Bookstore on High Street was below Emily's Typical Typing office, N. Emopee's typing service, and having just dropped off a new list of production company producers with Emily, he decided Hick's needed a quick look-see. Ostensibly, he was looking for a copy of the *Loomis' Street Guide to Hollywoods*, typically sold in used bookstores at half the price, despite being brand-new. Ambling up to the store, he noticed that the shade in the front display window was, once more, down tight, as it often was on a summer afternoon, the late-day sun bleaching the books white, otherwise. Through the amber screen the books looked floating in varnish.

With a grab of the glass front door, he was quickly inside, but not before his knee broke the beam of the security device, which Mr. Hick used at night to alert him of would-be burglars, and during the day of would-be customers, except that on a busy day the beep drove everybody crazy.

"Good afternoon, Mr. Emopee," Mr. Hick from the center of the front counter, his high-pitched voice as if he were pleading for his life. Hooked to his ears, by the look of it, or was it tied to the back of his head, a big black beard, which when he spoke swayed at his jaw like a mud flap.

"Good day, Mr. Hick," N. Emopee, as usual.

Which was when a low rumble under the counter suggested that Mr. Hick had missed his lunch, except that it was Bert, the old man's old dog, yawning or burping or whatever it did. It so happened that ten years earlier this shop was "Hick's Mutts, Used Dogs," a pet store where Mr. Hick sold dogs whose owners no longer wanted them. The business thrived in the beginning, the dog food he invented, "Mutt Mix," particularly successful. Even people liked eating it. The place, like a feed store, still smelled of it.

"I will not have a kennel, though" Mr. Hick would always say in self defense, but without a kennel that had a means of cleaning up after dogs, he was left with having to take his mutts for walks. This was, generally, four at a time, "to shit them," as he put it. But this turned out to be a complicated and time-consuming chore, by the end of it, "I'm not a young man anymore," so with the sale of his last dog, in came the books. He did not have to take books for a walk.

"How's Bert today?"

"Good afternoon, Mr. Emopee."

Mr. Hick was hard of hearing, to boot.

If N. Emopee's eyes rolled, it was to find again the gallery of hand-painted portraits surrounding the shop, pictures of writers past, Faulkner, Hemingway, Poe, for instance, painted according to Mr. Hick "by a friend of mine," even though they were all painted by him noticeably, because they all looked like him. If not a portraitist, Mr. Hick might well be a writer, for what more perfect arrangement could there be? His tiny apartment at the back of the store, on the second floor, accessed by a door beside Literary Criticism, was as convenient as it got. To get things going of a morning, he need only come downstairs for two minutes, long enough to let in his employees, who ran the place anyway, the remainder of his time free for scribbling stories.

But now, not spotting a *Loomis' Guide*, N. Emopee turned left at the first aisle and headed four sections over. Here was what, originally, was a coatroom, now Plato's Cave, so-called, the philosophy and religion section. It was, to be honest, the real reason N. Emopee was there. Plato's Cave held two hundred books, give or take twenty, but only two people, and as there were two already in there, the "gnome" Jules, and Raymond, Mr. Hick's gangly teenage grandson, it didn't look promising. Finding a customer suddenly in the doorway, however, and as good employees were instructed to do, Jules and Raymond yielded the space at once. A touch to their foreheads, as if seamen to a captain coming on deck, and off they went.

As it happened, Jules and Raymond left behind a cardboard box of no small size, which apparently they had been unloading, books newly acquired that day from the townspeople, and from the local college students. They were books for which Mr. Hick paid cash, or gave credit, neither amounting to much. The store sold its paperbacks at half price, and its hardcovers for little more, so that if Mr. Hick was to make a profit he could not purchase incoming books for more than 10 percent of their cover price. It was the source of more than one long face. In the end, though, "'Better than throwing the books away, I guess," most people concluded.

N. Emopee's attention went first to the shelf where the books he was watching for would be, only he came up empty again. This left the cardboard box in the middle of the floor. However, boxes had a way of betraying hopes too, and so it was that here once more he came up with nothing. "Did they come in and go out already, or did they merely not come in yet?" to himself tense-lipped. "Since when is everyone interested in mysticism?"

As this was the month, October, that the Director of Development job at CineProd was to materialize, N. Emopee sent a follow-up letter to Mr. Bucks and Mr. Gul. Depending on what they said, he was poised to mail follow-up notes to the other producers, whom, the last time around, wouldn't give him the cost of a stamp. Persistence was the name of the game in the Woods, according to Doh.

Two days later N. Emopee returned to Plato's Cave only to find that there were still no books on mysticism. Apropos of the subject, he supposed, "Now you see it, now you don't." But, then, the only thing that words could do was point at it, after all; they weren't it. It was like Taoism where the admonishment was, he who says he knows the Tao, does not; he who says he does not know the Tao, does know it. Or in Zen Buddhism where the great Zen Master Goen warned, "Books not Zen!" N. Emopee, as though these thoughts were solace to him, took a breath. On the other hand, what exactly did he need more books on mysticism for anyhow? The reason there were no more books on mysticism in Plato's Cave was because he had bought them all already. No, he was missing the point, was not being honest with himself about it. What he wanted was *It* itself, not more words about *It*. Buying, reading more books about *It*, though, was his way of remaining once removed from *It*, as though he feared *It*. The truth was, he had what he wanted already. He had *It*, and *It* had him, as far back as he could remember, to say nothing of his being "called" by *It* as recently as the past week.

Since being let go by the Stiff Arm Symphony, and becoming an even better oboist because of it, the trouble with the Third Chair, N. Emopee spent much of his time in his job-hunt war room. This was a brick-walled wine cellar behind the stone stairs on the path to the pomegranate trees behind his house. Joining him in the wine cellar was Cleo, a dwarf, "Call a spade a spade," she said, who lived in a camp down over the hill. Her favorite thing was collecting crow bones, oboe crow bones as she referred to them, the pomegranate trees a rookery. The birds craved the little pomegranate berries, even though, as they would be the first to admit if they could, getting them out of their pods was a royal pain in the beak.

Then, Cleo did not always collect crow bones. She once was a clockmaker. Indeed, her shop "Short on Time, Clox by Cleo" was a landmark in Morganhill, in the Old Stone House on Chestnut Street, an historic site now. She would have been more successful at the business had her clocks worked. She, it seemed, dreaded finishing things, dreaded dying, according to her therapist, and so her clocks, each in a handcrafted clock box, hence Clox, while they ticked up a storm, never quite made it to noon, much less to midnight. When she closed her shop eventually, she put a sign in the window, "Out of Time," and lived on pennies a month from Social Security.

N. Emopee had struck up a friendship with her three years earlier when he bought a jack-in-the-box clock from her, turn the crank and up popped the time. But when he found out that she was now living in a cardboard shack down by the railroad tracks, he invited her to take one of the empty rooms in his house. She need only keep an eye on things in return. She said she'd gladly live <u>at</u> his place but not <u>in</u> it, the dying thing again, hence her idea for a camp down in the grove.

Here, in late afternoon, N. Emopee was quaffing a carafe of his favorite wine, his homemade pomegranate port, when in came Cleo, her raven hair back in a bun and a bag full of bones on her back. "How goes the war?" the first words from her slack jaw.

"Which one?" N. Emopee, his lips getting a wipe with a sugar wafer, which he then popped down his throat in apparent delight.

"You'll get a headache from all that sugar, Nathan," Cleo, Cleoly.

Nathan? Except for Rem, Cleo was the only one who ever called him by his full first name. Eunice, his adopted mother, called him "dear."

"Would you like to see some bones?"

Before N. Emopee could answer, Cleo's latest collection was out on the table. N. Emopee looked on with interest. "What do you make of them, Cleo?" he said at last.

Years ago, to supplement her clock making business, Cleo mastered the I Ching, those sixty-four hexagrams consisting of full and broken lines, which Cleo imitated with full and broken crow bones. She used them to predict the future for anyone in need, for a price, naturally, ten dollars usually.

"Change is in the cards, in the bones, Nathan," Cleo, swiftly, N. Emopee still at her shoulder. "Change is afoot, in the foot bones."

"Spare me, Cleo."

Cleo, impishly resumed.

N. Emopee, meantime, knowing something of the hexagrams himself, "You know, of course, that Jesuit scholars studying the I Ching in China were declared heretics by the Vatican, so just give it to me straight, Cleo, or I'll tell the Pope on you."

Cleo scowled.

"When change comes, Nathan, you must be ready to seize the moment, to grab it with vigor and daring," word for word, to be safe, from the Legge translation. She peered at the bones more closely, with N. Emopee following her every movement. "Patience, though, Nathan, is the course of action for you just now. You must wait for events to be ready for you."

N. Emopee, back on his chair now with a creak, his lanky left leg over his right, to where his pulse bounced it up and down, "No waiting, Cleo. I've been without income for three months now, living on only my fading credit. I'm as good as evicted from here, no remnants of foreign wars for my dad, and you know what that means for me." He drew his right thumb across his throat.

Her heavy shoulders heaving, and then dropping just as heavily, Cleo, "The hexagrams tell you only what you should do, Nathan, not what you must do. Would you happen to have a cig on you?"

"You know I don't smoke cigarettes anymore, Cleo."

"You could have started again since I saw you last."

"Since an hour ago?"

"An hour is an eternity, Nathan."

"How about a cigar instead?"

"You know I don't smoke cigars anymore. How about a chew?"

"You know I don't chew tobacco anymore, Cleo. How about a bowl?"

"You know I don't smoke a pipe anymore, Nathan. How about a rub?"

"You know I don't rub snuff anymore, Cleo. How about a pomegranate port?"

"I thought you'd never ask."

Chapter Three
Meeting Bock and Snavely

*K*nown for his popular travelogue and wildlife TV series, Bill Bock was a familiar film and television producer in Los Angeles, and now here in the Woods as well, who had been, as N. Emopee learned on researching him, a child actor. This, of course, was before Bock's studies in business years later at USC in Los Angeles, following which he launched his production company, Telepic. That N. Emopee was nose-to-nose with him this day was Emily's doing, Emily of Typical Typing. She had met the producer while she and her girlfriend were sunbathing at the girlfriend's cottage on the river, a cottage next door to Bock's, it turned out. What Emily's friend looked like in a bikini N. Emopee did not know, but Emily would surely be an eyeful. She certainly would be for Bock, an infamous womanizer, a happy pants if ever there was one.

"When Mr. Bock came over and chatted with us last week," Emily to N. Emopee, "I told him that I had a customer who was having a terrible time getting into film and television, despite having superior qualifications."

"You don't say. Have him get in touch with me then," the producer, according to Emily, to which he added, "I like to give a kid a break, care to come over for a drink?"

Bock, at fifty years old, another fifty-year-old, apologized to N. Emopee when they met the following Friday morning, "You see, we're on hiatus this month," his informal attire, a shirt with a blue hibiscus bloom on the front of it, the evidence. His collar, meanwhile, open to reveal his child actor's smooth chest, was in marked contrast to his full head of straw-blond hair combed back to a duck's tail. He looked like Donnie Fargo of the pro wrestling circuit up in Pittsburgh.

"Hiatus?" N. Emopee's lack of familiarity with this biz term killed the interview right there, he feared.

His half glasses to his full nose, Bock was at N. Emopee's resume now, the same vita that Crump at Popcorn had photographed with a glance, with the exception that this one highlighted his, N. Emopee's, schooling, hence Bock's enthusiasm, "it says here that you went to USC. That's my alma mater, too, you know."

"I know," N. Emopee.

"As a matter of fact, I headed the fund drive for the alumni association there this past year."

Knowing nothing about college fund drives, N. Emopee remained mum, another strike against him?

"We have a good football team this year, don't you think? Do you like football?"

"Football?" N. Emopee was there for a job, not to tryout for the squad. Another strike?

"You must have gone to a lot of our home games over at the Coliseum," Bock, persisting, even as his eyes hunkered down once more on the resume. N. Emopee was careful not to interrupt what he hoped, at the finish, would be a thorough consideration, even though Bock, by the look of him, was not reading so much as dozing.

"If there's anything I can clarify--"

"You know," the producer, popping up at last, "I don't think I can help you."

N. Emopee, in case this happened, "I've been told I'm overqualified."

"Your words not mine, Mr. Emopee."

"N."

"Pardon me?"

"Never mind."

"The fact is, I have more oboists than I know what to do with just now."

"But oboing isn't--"

"But I'll tell you what. I'll think about it some more and get back to you. That Emily has some fine bazookas, huh?"

"Excuse me?"

Bock's half glasses fell on its cord onto the blue hibiscus bloom on the front of his shirt. "But if I do come up with something, it won't be with my company, I'm afraid." Slipping on his sandals now, Bock stepped to a pitcher of ice water at a side table and poured himself a quart. "The big studios have training programs, though," he went on with a chug, "a chance I could get you into one of those--although you might have to drive a truck for a while."

"Drive a truck, unload a truck--" N. Emopee, sighing.

"Have you thought of the ministry?"

N. Emopee stared.

It was a coincidence that Bock mentioned the ministry, because a brochure was stuck in his door that very morning. A brochure in his door wouldn't be out of the ordinary in his part of town except that it had his name on it, along with the words "Haven't we met before?"

That Bock said "ministry' to him out of the blue was strange enough, but now this? To say it was odd, creepy even, was an understatement, particularly as the pamphlet did not indicate from where or from whom it came, except that it had a cross on the front of it.

His first thought was that this was synchronicity, Jung's word for it, meaningful coincidence. Then again the same line, "Haven't we met before?" came from the producers at Popcorn and Famous Films, so synchronicity seemed unlikely. Still, it could be meaningful coincidence, he supposed. There were no hard fast rules on how, when or where it would occur, or what it would look like.

Another possibility was that it was a second step in the calling he experienced two weeks earlier, where the ground shook during his morning meditation. The Buddha had this happen to him all the time during his meditations. Whatever caused this with the Buddha caused it with him as well, as no doubt it happened to many meditators over the centuries. It was not God doing it, though, but the universe.

The third likelihood was that it was tathata, to use the Zen term for it, meaning that which is so of itself. Something just is. Zen used tathata in relation to the universe, speaking of which; the universe just is.

For N. Emopee it was getting on his nerves.

The willingness of the Woods' largest public television station to talk with him about employment was because he had just met their senior vice president at the Palace of Pump, a sports club he'd bought a lifetime membership to back when things were good for him. "Send me your resume," the v.p. to him as they lounged in the buff in the sauna, a place where the v.p. knew it unwise to provoke animosity. Indeed, he thought this new acquaintance, after subsequent reflection, would see it unfair of him to have raised the subject. Yet N. Emopee remained desperate for a job, frantic to return to the biz, remembering that he had worked at RBC television in Pittsburgh, a Remarkable Broadcasting Corporation stagehand-of-the month, at one point, in fact, preceded by plumber-of-the-month, albeit this time looking for a different capacity altogether. Which was why he appeared at the v.p.'s office door the first thing the next morning. "The postal system is so slow with resumes," he said.

Unfortunately Mr. Snavely was a budget man, finance the last thing N. Emopee was qualified for, with the result that he was not with Snavely for very long. The station's Miscellaneous Department was where he wound up.

A large lady in her small thirties, red hair and lipstick to match, the Miscellaneous Director seemed physically uncomfortable five minutes into their talk, no earthly reason why, not that N. Emopee could think of anyway, unless it was flatulence, not uncommon in public television. Eventually, he sensed that it was because she wanted to get rid of him, not too quickly at first, as not to offend Mr. Snavely, with whom she wished to maintain smooth relations, but rid of him, all the same. "What exactly are you looking for, Mr. Emopee?"

N. Emopee pulled himself up. "What have you got?"

The woman tightened her tight brow even tighter, whereupon her eyes fell to his waiting vita. In the meanwhile, the pine shelf on the wall just behind her caught N. Emopee's attention, a series of awards standing there nakedly, metal figurines, all in gold. Oscars they weren't, leaving him to conclude that they were trophies from her son's Little League baseball team. He made to ask.

"I know," the woman, looking up all of a sudden, began, "that you are not looking for oboing but a career change, but it says here that you are the only one ever to successfully interpret Schuler's *Concerto Number 6, Opus 3, for Oboe and Tambourine*. Is this so?"

"That was a long time ago. Is it still on my resume?" N. Emopee peered over.

"I know how difficult that piece is, being a tambourinist myself." Noticeably more relaxed now, the lady was almost giddy.

"You don't say."

"It's what I do for fun."

"Oh?"

"Just between us musicians, my secret ambition is Widge's *Symphony Tambourique for Solo Tambourine*."

N. Emopee, "I've never heard of it."

"Of course, you haven't."

N. Emopee wasn't sure how to take this. Then, again, being an oboist he knew what obscurity was. The woman looked once more at to his resume.

"It lists here everything you can play, all in one sitting. That's an amazing repertoire you have. Why do you want to give it up?"

N. Emopee straightened, then leaned back. "Well, honestly, between us musicians, I've played that repertoire for so many years that I've forgotten it," not the truth of it really, like riding a bicycle, once you can ride it you always can, but he didn't want his distance vision, or lack thereof, to become their focus, so to say, although the thickness of his glasses had to tell her something. He leaned forward, once again, but not before an espresso cart came rattling down the hall. Next to pomegranate port, he loved caffe macchiatos.

"Well, it seems to me," the woman, at last, "if you want to be in the film and television business you might go for story analysis. Story analysts evaluate scripts for film and television based on their dramatic qualities, which should be right up your alley. It says here that you have dramatic tendencies."

N. Emopee liked it. "I like it," he said.

"Unfortunately, we don't employ readers, as they are called, here, beyond what I do myself, naturally."

"Naturally."

"But most everyone else in town uses them, union or free-lance. You'd have to get someone to train you, though."

Train him? Wasn't he trained already? "How do I get someone to train me?"

Now on her hefty feet, the lady turned behind her to the shelf with all the trophies. She picked up the nearest one. "By getting a lucky break, Mr. Emopee, like everyone else in this business."

N. Emopee, "Aren't you my lucky break?"

The lady placed the gold figurine back on the shelf. "Have you ever played women's softball?"

N. Emopee blinked.

"I am only your first break, Mr. Emopee. Just keep doing what you're doing, send letters, meet people. Have you ever thought of the priesthood?"

N. Emopee rolled his eyes.

The bad news was that he left the public TV station still without a job, the good news, that he had a definition now, story analyst, a major accomplishment at that.

In the meantime, sets were being built for a TV series about the planets, or so explained the guide parading tourists past the scene shop near where N. Emopee was departing. The Masonite moon and Styrofoam stars made him nostalgic for his old stagehand job in Pittsburgh, hauling scenery in the beginning, hanging it in the end, sentimental regarding his life up north generally, not all this anxiety for him back then, what had he gotten himself into?

What he'd gotten himself into, of course, was the great expectations game, where his recent success in the concert hall had everyone wondering what he would accomplish next, with none more curious than himself, even as most were surprised, if not disappointed, that he did not go into college teaching like his dad, even though he, N. Emopee, never had the slightest interest in it, and arguably lacked the temperament for it.

"Swear," N. Emopee's father had demanded of him on his deathbed. Swear? It rather seemed a raw deal to N. Emopee. Where was the fairness in it? Yet, N. Emopee could not now, of clear conscience, turn around and hand it off to the next generation, to N. Emopee junior, if and when there was ever a junior, which was not likely anytime soon.

Announcing to his adopted mother that he was getting back into film and television, in a bigger way than ever this time, not as a stagehand but as a story analyst, was a big mistake. "Foolishness," was her reaction. "If you don't want to teach at the community college like your father, then you should at least be a technician," that merciless job N. Emopee promised himself never to submit to, despite its chasing him over the years, and which possibly he still might wind up doing despite everything, even though it would give him a heart attack.

Cable television was the wave of the future, N. Emopee read the next day in both *The Hollywoods Reporter* and the *Daily Vanity,* and so he sent ten letters with resume to cable TV executives, on the off chance that one of them would train him to be a story analyst.

"Script," came the firm voice on the other end of the line, as if a producer were calling to strike a deal with him. This was Saul Script, one of two Hollywoods screenwriters that N. Emopee had taken a course from following the drama class he had that time, not with the idea of becoming a screenwriter but to compare screenplays with stage plays, like in his drama class. He was curious.

"Hello, Mr. Script?" N. Emopee, unevenly. "You may not remember me, but my name is N. Emopee, one of your students in your screenwriting class a few years back, six years ago to be precise."

Script's voice fell to a whisper. "Yeah, sure, N. You're the oboist. What have you been up to?"

"Well, funny you should ask. Well, not funny-funny, but you see I'm trying to get into story analysis for film and television here in the Woods, and I thought you might have some advice for me."

A deeper silence.

"Hello?"

"I'm here," Script.

How many times in how many ways had his former students asked him over the years. Everybody wanted into the biz.

"I was told that I should start as a free-lance analyst and go from there. Is this a good idea?"

"Don't you want to be an oboist any longer?"

"My conductor looks like the Milky Way to me, I'm sad to say. My eyesight's shot."

"Why don't you sit closer in?"

N. Emopee, a shrug, "I'm already closer in, or was. I can't sit in the conductor's lap."

"Well, you can be an analyst if you like, N.," Script, after a minute. "I've done it myself. But I don't recommend it."

"Why?"

"There's not enough money in it."

"I thought I might do it just to get started, to get my foot in the door, so to say, money no object," not the truth of it, of course, "just to see how it goes."

"You can do it if you want, N., like I said, but just don't expect to make a living at it."

"Would you happen to know anyone who might take me on, give me a chance at it, train me, if you don't mind my asking?" the other shoe Script was waiting to hear drop. "You get asked this all the time, I'll bet," N. Emopee dribbled on. "At least twice a day, I imagine."

"Sometimes," Script, frankly; "sometimes I get asked all the time." But then, "Homer Tank at the OBC story department might help you out. You can use my name."

"The Omnipotent Broadcasting Corporation?" N. Emopee dashed this down, along with the name Homer Tank, only to jabber on at Script for ten minutes longer, without taking a breath, without coming up for air, showing his appreciation, until, at last, Script's keyboard pecking in the background signaled that N. Emopee's time was up.

"Thanks a million, Mr. Script.

Script, "Let me know when it dawns on you who you really are."

N. Emopee lowered the receiver slowly.

House painting again for his uncle, Eunice's younger brother, did not at first occur to him. His big break, that big job in the biz, would appear any day now, so why should he commit to painting if he was going to start his new career the very next day? Now that he was in financial straits, though--

Rufus had been semi-retired since the first of the year, carrying just enough work for himself, small jobs, mainly. As it happened, Rufus found that he did not like painting by himself, a lonely affair, and doing only small jobs that did not make him any money. Also, despite his customers' knowledge that he was semi-retired, they continued to call him for entire houses, 5-painter size jobs, which Rufus hated to turn down, which was to say, he hated turning down all those bucks.

A contractor in Morganhill for forty years, Rufus didn't look like a painter. With square jaw, sandy hair, what was left of it, and lean hips, he looked more a football coach than a painter. He had first taught N. Emopee the painting trade when he, N. Emopee, was eighteen years old, or his men had shown him anyway. After that, N. Emopee filled in with it, as he needed to, even in Pittsburgh prior to his employment at RBC television.

Of course, he hadn't painted since he'd become an oboist, so going back to it these years later wasn't an easy decision for him to make. Still he had to have work of some kind, he knew, if for only a few days each week, just enough to pay his bills. Maybe his morale would get a boost along with it, his continuing unemployment taking its toll on his normally hopeful spirit.

"So let me know if you can use me," N. Emopee, over the phone to Rufus.

He started the next morning.

With the success of his call to Saul Script, N. Emopee decided to contact CineProd again, that Director of Development job having developed firmly by now. He wanted to tie up that loose end, if indeed it was loose anymore. If it wasn't, they might have a story analyst position for him, or be willing to train him at it. "Hello, may I speak with Tru Bucks or Mo Gul?"

"Mr. Bucks and Mr. Gul are no longer with us," the receptionist, quickly to him. "Our new corporate owners have cut back on staff, and have downsized to where, in fact, we are moving our offices off the MGM lot this very week."

"Off of the Metro Goldwyn Mayer lot?"

"Off the Morganhill Goodwin Monroe lot."

"You wouldn't know whether there's a Director of Development position available anymore, would you?"

"A what?"

This left Bill Bock.

"I'm sorry, Mr. Bock is not in today," his secretary to N. Emopee, softly. "May I take a message?"

"This is Mr. N. Emopee. Would you tell him that I inquired regarding employment, whether he had anything for me yet, a training program or anything?"

"Mr. Bock sold his cottage on the river, Mr. Emopee."

Chapter Four
Omnipotent Broadcasting Corporation

"Who'd have guessed it?" Jon Doh at the AFI library, that day's Hollywoods Reporter and Daily Vanity in his hands.

"But I didn't want to work in schlock," N. Emopee, his hands in the air, "didn't want to give Crump my drama class paper, something for nothing, didn't want to unload trucks, or be a fried assistant."

"You what?"

Both trade papers were heralding the suddenly booming business at Popcorn Pictures, million dollar deals signed and sealed, big flicks in the works, big bucks for everyone. N. Emopee sagged. A call back to Crump was possible, he supposed, on the odd chance that Crump would still let him in. On the other hand, what if he did sign with Popcorn, as a low paid assistant, for example, only to have a major position at a major studio suddenly come pouncing onto his plate? He couldn't then drop Crump again. This was how people got a bad reputation in the biz. Still, he asked himself, what was the probability of such a job at one of the majors any time soon?

He sighed.

Doh sighed, too.

Then, it was a roller coaster ride from the very beginning, as evidenced by a letter waiting for him when he got back to his office. Theona Windle, the Western Regional Director at Entertainment Cable, cable television, said that she had forwarded his resume to their corporate headquarters in St. Louis and that a position for him was "likely," that they needed a story analyst, to be trained by them. They would be in touch.

Regrettably, it was the worst time of year to be painting houses in Morganhill, temperatures remaining over 100 degrees, the Fairfield winds again, and the air, well, on his first day on the job he found that he couldn't stop coughing. Smog in Morganhill of all places. The L.A. Hollywood must have brought the smog with it. Rufus, however, insisted they tough it out, so he could get paid.

"Fire me if you want," the wheezing N. Emopee; "I'm outa here."

Well, N. Emopee was not let go, not just yet anyway, even though he and Rufus were off to a shaky start.

But then why should he, N. Emopee, put up with this anyhow, he asked himself once again? Why not go back to Hieronymus Hup at the Stiff Arm Symphony, or to Byron Tossemoff at the Embouchure Ensemble across the river in Westhill? With his reputation as a third oboist, certainly they would have <u>something</u> for him. He could be, at the very least, a music page turner.

Well, the answer was simple enough. His distance vision was not the issue with them any longer. It seemed he had forfeited his ever working again for Stiff Arm by his seeking employment in film and television. The word was out on him. The music world had blacklisted him for it, "behavior unbecoming a Stiff Armian," musicians a conservative lot. It was a penalty he did not expect, not quite, anymore than, to be honest, the blacklisters themselves expected to levy.

N. Emopee's newest malady did not help. It seems his left ring finger, either from disuse or from years of overuse, had arched terribly, much like his dad's had from selling running shoes, so that now were he to get lucky and to play the oboe again, he would be missing F sharp.

The familiar clank of a paint can lid in the garage evidenced that Ed, N. Emopee's Buddhist house painter, was cleaning up after his day on the fence. N. Emopee knew quite a lot about this Ed, even though he was face to face with him rarely. He knew, for example, that he had a doctorate in philosophy, a doctor of philosophy in philosophy degree, but who had, in Ed's words to him only a week before, grown past this, opting instead for what he considered a more direct way of experiencing life. There was nothing theoretical about painting a house, he said. Paint on his hands was not an abstraction. N. Emopee knew exactly what he was talking about.

These days Ed mostly painted the vast fence surrounding the house, they had to keep up appearances, which he offered to do at minimal charge, in exchange for other better-paying work that N. Emopee promised him in the months ahead. As for painting all the way around the winding fence, only to start over again, Ed must have found it monotonous and boring, but Ed said he didn't mind it. For him it was a Buddhist meditation point, life as a cycle.

Intercepting Ed this evening crossed N. Emopee's mind, a chat with him perhaps, except that Ed did not chat, and anyway it was late, and Ed would be tired. N. Emopee was tired, too. And besides, Ed would surely ask him once more about the peeling siding on the west side of the house, to say nothing of the walls in the living room. He would want to know whether N. Emopee wanted them painted anytime soon, which again, this month, N. Emopee would have to decline.

The Omnipotent Broadcasting Corporation story department was located on the second floor of an olive-green house on Olive Road in New Burbank east of Morganhill. At non-rush hour, it took N. Emopee's blimp-of-a-station wagon thirty minutes one way to get there, and round trip, more gasoline than he could afford. Yet as he sat stiffly in his blimp across the street, waiting for the hour of his appointment, he could only hope it was worth the effort. True, Homer Tank's secretary had told him on the phone that they had no reader openings just then, "But Mr. Tank is willing to talk with you just the same," she said, the result of N. Emopee's dropping the name of Saul Script.

As OBC supposedly had no job openings, the best N. Emopee could hope for was another name, someone else who might take him on as, in this case, a trainee. "People could go for years at this," he huffed, his hard chin getting a tug. Not one to own a watch, he cranked on his radio to get the local time from the Woods' all-news local station, KNW, KNOW RADIO. "10:41 a.m.," it barked, which meant that there were nineteen minutes to go.

A confounding configuration, this. The Green Bag Road, or the Green-Back Road, as detractors of the biz had it, had just been renamed Olive Road. This connected to Lost Dog Road, Crow Road, Bent Cat Road, and Suck Hole Road, now Suck Hole Parkway. Like airport runways, at all angles, they formed a single intersection somehow, with the OBC studio complex, the airport terminal, smack in the middle. Meantime, the drone of the ceaseless traffic had N. Emopee's already edgy nerves even more so.

This was a far cry from when OBC was the Robert F. Ard Federal Correctional Facility for Boys. "Bob's Box," as it was called, was vacated abruptly three years ago when all the boys ran one way and all the guards the other. God knew what happened, but the emptying of the facility couldn't have been timed better for OBC, which had just opened an office down on Ritchie Bordeaux Way, but which still needed a place to put its studios. And for the locals it was either OBC or another prison, and they had had enough of lockups.

Having to roll his window down for fresh air, diesel smoke hardly fresh air, N. Emopee more miserable still, for it was fresh <u>heat</u> as well. At 10:45 in the morning it was 90 degrees outside already, more of the desert winds. He could close the window and click on his air conditioner, naturally, but long ago he learned his lesson on that one, had the watery eyes and sore throat from the force-feeding of smog. Then there were the five gallons of gasoline the air conditioner burned up each time, which, in the best of times, his wallet could ill handle.

"10:50 a.m.," KNW, along with their jingle once more, and his minutes to go were down to ten.

N. Emopee's twitching eyes turned now to the olive-green house before him there on Olive Road, at his side window before him, or was the house apple green? Better yet it was jade green, and with its broad flared roof, he imagined it a Japanese temple. Ananda, the Buddha's favorite disciple, sat in the office on the first floor, surely, except that, when finally at 11:00 N. Emopee strode in to find Dick Clark instead.

A carpeted stairway, beige, stretched steeply to his left here, to the second floor, where the story department secretary could be seen at her desk, and whom N. Emopee reached in eight bounding thuds. She was finishing business on the phone, he could see, this African-American with the oversize horn rim glasses, cherry red, concluding business even though it sounded less like business than girlfriend chatter.

As he had in Crump's office at Popcorn Pictures, N. Emopee, seated now, calmed himself by focusing on the carpet in front of him, another oriental affair, but this one with no mandala in the center of it, just plum blossoms, lots of plum blossoms.

But now in the next minute his eyes were on his clothing. Was he was dressed properly? Did he have on the right tie, the right shoes, the right belt, first impressions being everything, even in the biz, especially in the biz. He would have worn his deep blue silk suit again, except that the silkworm-rights activists were back in town, and anyway he didn't want to appear too formal, didn't want to look too oboish. Overly casual was not good either, as if he didn't take the appointment seriously.

He had thought of wearing what he supposed a story analyst would wear, until he realized he didn't know what this was exactly; he'd never seen a story analyst before, except for Saul Script, and he dressed like a screenwriter did, faded jeans, black t-shirt, and a corduroy sport jacket. In the end, he wore what he *imagined* a story analyst wore, if, say, he were writing one into a novel, brown loafers, blue slacks, a dark blue short-sleeve shirt with wispy white and red lines forming checks, and a brown knit tie.

Seeing him contemplating himself, the secretary grinned a broad grin all at once, whereupon the receiver slipped from her delicate ear and slid, with a soft ta-click, onto its waiting stand. With a shake of her short black hair, and a smoothing of her purple print blouse, she decided to get right to it: "You must be Mr. N. Emopee," an ultra slim cigarette to her ultra slim mouth. "Sorry to keep you waiting."

"How do you do?" N. Emopee was careful not to thrust out his hand, etiquette being etiquette.

"My name is Rayshal. Rayshal Lamary."

"No doubt it is," N. Emopee, although now he was searching his pockets for a match. Which was when he recalled that he no longer carried matches, having given up cigarettes six months prior.

"Mr. Tank will be with you in a moment," Rayshal, flattered all the same by the apparent offer of a light, said. A touch of her desk lighter promptly did the deed. "He's with one of our readers at the moment you see. In fact, it was another of our readers I was just speaking with on the phone. Like family we are around here, you know."

N. Emopee didn't know, but he would like to. He would also like to know more about this voice of Rayshal's, her velvety contralto, with its impeccable diction, every bit the actor's. It reminded him of Crump's personal secretary Mabelondra, the Space Shenanigan, so that his eyes searched the walls for a Rayshal poster.

"Are you looking for something?" The secretary was following his eyes again.

N. Emopee glanced back. "A job," he smiled. Just then a tall young man stepped briskly from Tank's office. He was wearing brown loafers, blue slacks, a dark blue short sleeve shirt with wispy white and red lines forming checks, and a knit tie, brown.

Unlike N. Emopee's adopted mother Eunice, Ed the painter did not call the house a--what did Eunice call it?--a shack. Ed, if he called it anything, called it a windmill. A windmill? Pieter Bruegel, the sixteenth century Flemish artist, had a windmill tittering precariously on a high crag in the background of his "Carrying of the Cross."

N. Emopee's dad was obsessed with making the house the same thing, the sails still laid out in the garage. And for sure he had the crag part right. The house was perched atop what was once Dorsey's Knob, an ancient outcropping of rock high above Morganhill. It was visible for miles around. Even on Ritchie Bordeaux Way down over the hill, it could be seen.

The only thing N. Emopee knew about Bruegel was his combining of locations, Jerusalem and Flanders, for instance, in that "Carrying of the Cross" picture.

Mr. Tank did not get up from his desk when Rayshal introduced N. Emopee to him, a toad on a rock to see him. Another fifty-year-old, he wore a maroon shirt, parted at the collar to reveal his three chins, and charcoal slacks.

His lack of deodorant, though, made the room smell like a gymnasium. "Have a seat, Mr. Emopee," he poked.

As N. Emopee took the nearby chair, in his hands suddenly was a page entitled ELEMENTS, a sheet whose significance he recognized immediately, and which he ogled with instantly twitching brow. What followed then was a half hour lecture by Tank on story analysis for television and film.

Was there some mistake? Did Tank think that he, N. Emopee, was somebody else, even though he had just called him by name? But then at the conclusion of the talk his great good fortune was confirmed. He was handed a script, 118 pages, with the instructions, "Here's one to get your feet wet, to cut your teeth on, to learn the ropes with. Write a 'coverage' from what I've described on that page, and if it's satisfactory, I'll give you a better one the next time."

Then, as though a part of OBC training, if not a rite of entry, Tank launched into his personal history, all about how he had started in the biz as a cable puller, which was a guy who pulled the TV camera cable out of the way of the camera wheels during taping, then as a cameraman himself, becoming, eventually, a technical director, the one in charge of all the cameras. From there, he took the head position, not only of the technical direction office, but of the staging and design offices as well, to say nothing of the office of costuming and makeup. He was winding up his career there in the story department. With forty-seven years in broadcasting, twenty-three of them at OBC, he was looking forward to retirement soon, he confessed, "as soon as a successor to me can be found."

Forty-seven years? This meant that Tank would have started in the biz at the age of three. There were young cable pullers, and then there were young cable pullers!

Tank plowed through N. Emopee's resume next, to refresh his memory. "Our analysts come from every background," he noted, "all of whom have gone on to do quite well for themselves, moving up the ladder here at OBC, or becoming executives with other companies. As for your background, Mr. Emopee--" At the end of the vita now, Tank paused, then lifted his left eyebrow.

"I've been told I'm overqualified," N. Emopee, not knowing really what this pause was about, bracing himself for the worst, though.

Tank drew back just as N. Emopee drew forward.

"Goose poop," Tank, then, firmly.

N. Emopee drew back.

"No one is overqualified to be a reader at OBC, not even your friend Script, who happens to have a Ph.D. in film, you know."

N. Emopee did not know this, reminding himself that after all he had known Script only briefly, during only one of Script's courses, and at no time was the writer ever referred to by his students, or by anyone else that he knew of, as Dr. Script.

At the same time, wasn't it precisely what he wanted to hear from Tank, that he, N. Emopee, was not out of place in this try of his for the biz, that despite his accomplishment as a third oboist, he was just as suited to be a story analyst as the next guy. Indeed, didn't he feel vindicated by it, feel victorious even, over the American Oboe Association on whose blacklist he remained for doing just this, seeking work in the biz, as well as over his mother Eunice who thought all this show biz stuff was just rubbish.

"A reader should be in this department no more than one year," Tank now, with a grunt, "the point at which he can expect to advance to the next level." What Tank did not say, however, and what N. Emopee was on the edge of his seat to hear him say, was that *he, N. Emopee*, could expect to advance in only one year, even though he hadn't even been hired yet.

Emily's Typical Typing was located three short blocks from N. Emopee's office on High Street. So it was that again this day he made the ten-minute trek to the steep stairs in the Lou D. Bang Building, where as always on the second floor, at the head of the steps, he heard Emily's typical typewriter pecking away.

As he moved along the second-floor hall he noted, once more, how it was laid in low-pile carpeting, dark green in color as not to show the dirt, and low pile so no one would trip, break his leg and sue Mr. Bang. Over his head, meantime, were three skylights, the 1940s peeked-style, metal frames with wire-reinforced diffused glass. While illuminating the way, they also highlighted the odd frankly forgettable picture, a tree on a hill, apples in a dish, and a dog.

But now N. Emopee was always perplexed by the absence of other humanity here, six businesses but never anyone around. "Where is everybody?" to Emily more than once. "Everybody?" Emily, each time. "Other office workers, customers, <u>anybody</u>." "Oh, they're around," Emily, a cryptic wink, her deep green eyes dancing blankly. Moonlighting businesses N. Emopee was left to conclude, or real estate or insurance companies where the agents were "out in the field" all the time. The company names didn't help any: The Company; Associates, Inc.; We-R-You, Ltd., among them.

In Emily's office now, N. Emopee noted how the letter carrier had just been through. Everyone it seemed had given up on deodorant.

Yet, if the odor bothered him, it didn't bother Emily, seemingly, for "'Right with you, hon," her cheery greeting once again, just as, with a sudden surge, she poked out the long, last paragraph on the page.

Hon? N. Emopee was still not used to it, even though he had heard it from her for a month now. Did he look like a hon?

With a clickety-clack then, or was it a tickety-tick, Emily completed what turned out to be a long paragraph, indeed, her skinny hands dropping into her lap then, as if they'd fallen off.

With auburn hair to the middle of her back Emily looked not at all the stereotypical small- town secretary-typist, pale and fat. As though in defiance of it, in fact, she wore tight-fitting slacks, a small bra, and sandals, which her customers, most of them anyway, enjoyed he was sure. He enjoyed it.

If N. Emopee had a complaint about her, though, it was that her eyes were too far apart, making it hard to see her, completely, in one look, two attempts to get it done.

For Emily, meanwhile, it had been sufficient to type the names of Hollywoods production companies onto envelopes. She liked it, was pleased to be a part of it. But now that morning she had, for the first time, typed an actual coverage, so-called, for an actual television script, N. Emopee having explained to her how it must be done exactly in the format Tank had provided him, including the centering of the header, "OBC NETWORK TELEVISION, Story Department, New Burbank."

Then, again, Emily had no small knowledge of this customer of hers, having typed, to date, forty of his cover letters with resume, where he attempted to sell himself except that she got sold in the process. Evidence her confession to him the last time that she had just broken up with her live-in boy friend of over a week now, although she stopped short of saying that she liked the sound of Emily Emopee.

Another feature about him that intrigued her was that little earring in his left earlobe. Sailors who rounded the "Horn," Cape Horn at the southern tip of South America, wore just such an earring in just this earlobe, sexy certainly, even though she hadn't the courage yet to ask him about it. It so happened, N. Emopee sported it for the same achievement, in his case rounding the French Horn out on the end of the fourth row at the Stiff Arm Symphony.

Taking his business to another of the local secretarial services would solve N. Emopee's discomfort with Emily's attraction to him, which he was well aware of, except that she gave him good prices, was nearby, and, well, wasn't pale and fat.

"Are you going to be sending out more letters with resume, or is that it, hon? Will it be coverages from here on?"

"Well, I don't know yet. I'd like it to be coverages, but my better judgment tells me that my letters with resume have to keep going out. I'll bring you a new list tomorrow. Until I've nailed down the OBC work, I've got to keep myself out there. I'm desperate, you could say."

"I'd never have guessed you the type, hon."

"What, desperate?"

"No, Hollywoods."

"What's wrong with Hollywoods?"

"I just never would have guessed it, that's all," a stick of spearmint gum into Emily's plush mouth with a curl.

"I'm not convincing, huh, not good at the part?"

Emily took a quick breath, more of a gasp, sensing she'd hit a nerve.

"To see ourselves as others see us, huh?" N. Emopee, as if he wasn't convinced of it either, shot back. "I shouldn't have you type these coverages then, if you think I'm not believable."

"Let's drop it, shall we?"

"Well, if I don't look like I'm the Hollywoods type, what do I look like?" his hands on his hips.

"Let's forget it, shall we?"

N. Emopee shook his head from side to side, then nodded resolutely to a stop.

"Besides, what difference would it make if I told you what you look like?" Emily, summing up. "Your mind is already made up."

"I should be what I look like I am maybe. I'd be hired in a minute."

Emily, swallowing shallowly, returned her hands to her machine, but not before handing N. Emopee the coverage she had typed for him earlier. "Let me know if you have more of these, hon. In the meantime, I'll bill you, okay?"

N. Emopee, turning slowly, "Fair enough." He then marched for the door, a sudden glance back as he reached it. "You still haven't told me what I look like I am."

Emily sighed, then resumed typing.

"Well?"

"You look like a monk, hon. A monk."

Chapter Five
Biz Sickness

N. Emopee kept at house painting for the time being. Rufus, though, was upset. When he learned of the development at OBC, all the story analyst training, he feared that the five fat contracts he had just committed to were in jeopardy now, houses which, without his nephew to help him, would be impossible to complete. This was to say, if N. Emopee left him at this point, he would have to hire another painter, or more, and likely at a higher wage, or would have to refer the work to another contractor, not what this was about, not what making him money was about.

Then, N. Emopee had no intention of leaving his uncle high and dry like that, not just yet anyway, despite his stipulating from day one that he would drop painting the minute he got hired in the biz. It was a condition that Rufus did not, it looked now, take seriously, even less so with the passing of time. He believed that if his nephew had not been hired in the biz yet, he never would be. Tension between them remained high.

"I think you should get into video," Tank to N. Emopee when, the next day, N. Emopee delivered his coverage to him. As it happened that there was a major article about the new technology in not only *The Hollywoods Reporter* but in the *Daily Vanity* as well. N. Emopee's coverage, in the meanwhile, got a quick look, a brisk scan by Tank, who then deemed it "fine."

Fine? Considering the eight hours N. Emopee put into it, as his inaugural one, he felt that it deserved more than a "fine," it didn't have to be cartwheels. His assurance that a full-time job was likely now would be nice. At the same time he looked for a sign that Tank would swivel on his rock and grab another script from the pile behind him, except that all Tank seemed interested in was talking some more about himself.

"Well, I'll tell you what," Tank, after another fifteen minutes, and noticing N. Emopee's glazed eyes, "I have two fourteen-page story proposals I can let you have. They're twenty-five bucks a piece, if you want them. It's all I can spare just now. I have to keep enough for my regulars, you know."

"Your regulars?"

"You may as well know that I have four per diem free-lancers," Tank pulling the proposals away from him just at the last moment, N. Emopee on the floor nearly. "One of them makes her living at it somehow, while the other three, well, I don't think there's enough money in it for them to make it worth their while. I don't see them all that often, though. Still, they do come around."

"They do, yes, of course." N. Emopee would too.

Which was when Tank hauled from the floor a twelve-pound dumbbell, which he proceeded to pump twelve times with his right arm, as if inflating a balloon. What an odd thing for an obese person to do, N. Emopee thought to himself. Tank could have a heart attack.

"The big picture is this, Mr. Emopee," Tank, out of breath already. "One of my people here in the office is not working out well for me, so I plan to send him to another department. This means that I'll have a full-time staff position available here soon."

N. Emopee raised his hand. "If--"

"You will be among those considered, Mr. N. Emopee, I assure you. You see, I like oboists, even confused ones."

That night, N. Emopee brought all his forces to bear on those two defenseless little story proposals, as if his life depended on them, which it did.

N. Emopee missed his adopted sister April, not seeing or speaking with her for ages now. April remained in Pittsburgh, in her secure job at Crucifix Regional, where she taught high school biology. She was, to use her term for it, a PPG, a professional paper grader, but also a professional papal grader, Crucifix a Catholic school, of course. April converted to Catholicism by way of her second husband, Luigi, despite her love of atheism. At least one of them was a teacher, N. Emopee shrugged to himself, if only to please their adopted mother. If, though, he missed his sister, it didn't change that he was jealous of her, April so conventional, such a perfectly adapted creature, a mole to a hole.

Then April was envious of her kid brother, too. He could accomplish anything he took an interest in, seemingly, sooner or later beating the odds against him, to where, for instance, he even became a third oboist.

Whatever negative feelings they had toward each other, didn't change that they were brother and sister, though, sort of. They were, after all, the offspring of Rem and Eunice Emopee, of "Peg Leg" and "Muzz," as they jokingly called their parents between the two of them, as if Rem and Eunice were cartoon characters, which they were after a fashion, as all parents are to their children at one time or another, and vice versa, especially if the family is dysfunctional.

As for telephoning his sister, what this moment was all about, N. Emopee was reluctant, all of a sudden, to go through with it. His continuing lack of success in the Woods was the culprit, a desperate, intolerable, embarrassing condition that frankly was driving him nuts, even though April would find it refreshing. No, he would have to think a while longer about phoning her. Maybe for her birthday in--he forgot.

With the left turn at Dick Clark's office, N. Emopee, his latest coverages in tow, was back up the angular steps to Rayshal, who informed him that Mr. Tank was busy that morning, that he could see him only momentarily.

"They're fine," Tank, with a brief look once again, his right bicep getting another pump with the dumbbell, physical therapy, N. Emopee settled on, bicep-replacement-rehab perhaps. "Submissions remain slow. I'll be in touch."

Down the hall N. Emopee ambled then, to get paid for the short reports, twenty-five bucks a piece from petty cash, meaningless to him considering the effort he'd put into them, the gasoline it took for him to get all the way back over there, and, finally, the cost of having Emily type them up. She charged him more for these pieces, more than for the letters with resume, because this was for OBC. She assumed that he was making a sizeable sum from his association with the network, an impression he let stand because he was too embarrassed to admit that it was quite the contrary.

The uncertainty of OBC, and then the collapse of his teaching aspirations a while back, were taking their toll on N. Emopee, so that even the change from Daylight Savings Time back to Standard Time upset him all to pieces. The shorter days were a reminder to him that he still was not a story analyst, only a story-analyst trainee, and that without a regular salary since the Stiff Arm Symphony, he really was in dire straits. Thank God for Rufus' house painting.

Rem died of over-education, thanks to his brief teaching stint at Sourbrook Community College east of Morganhill, whereupon Eunice happily moved out of the big house. She lived now in a very small house, comparatively. Visiting her there at Christmas, N. Emopee put on a happy face despite everything, appeared confident, seemed pleased by his progress in the biz, all a big show, regrettably. He had no reason to lie to her this way, of course, as if she didn't know who he was. Their conversation was at cross purposes as a result.

"I'm not sure when I'll get back over here to visit you," N. Emopee, frankly. "My new full-time job in show business will not include days off the first year."

"It's only a ten-minute drive, dear. Teachers have the entire summer off, six weeks in the winter." Eunice was still on the teaching thing.

"The recession has been tough on the film and TV industry, though, you know," N. Emopee, still on the biz. "But they're predicting a turnaround next year, more work, more jobs."

"Your sister was smart to get on at that high school," Eunice then said. "Teachers have security for life."

"But everyone sacrifices in show biz at first," pointed out N. Emopee. "Everybody struggles in the beginning."

"In the beginning? Why are you forever starting over, dear?"

Touché. Stagehand, plumber, oboist, and now story analyst. He was a walking job fair.

Jones Avenue on the hillside above Eunice's house, remembering that Morganhill rested in a long low valley, was where he went for meditation when he was over that way. The entire town, from Evansdale up the river to the right, to First Ward in the opposite direction, to downtown Morganhill, was visible from there. Shop-lined High Street, where he had his office, was in the crisp foreground. Readily recognizable in the distance, Sourbrook Community College. On the horizon, stuck high on that odd crag, looking every bit like that painting by Bruegel, his house at One Pound Down Street.

It brought to his mind that time eight years earlier when he left Morganhill, was expelled from Morganhill, and from all of West Virginia, for that matter, over his opposition to the latest Hayfields and McCays war. With a ravenous roar, the twin-engine Otter lifted him abruptly over the Morganhill airport, where, after a minute, it banked steeply to the north, rows of bare blue trees standing motionless below like soldiers of the Union holding a line.

Climbing for the cold winter clouds, the plane tipped now to the left, affording him a bird's eye view of the whole river valley. There in the corner he spotted Rem on the front steps of the house, waving stoically to him goodbye. N. Emopee waved back, knowing that Rem could not see him, which was just as well, for the tear in his eye.

For the next several moments the plane was in thick deep clouds, still ascending, until, at last, it cleared the final layer, a submarine surfacing in the Arctic, it felt like. Here, the light was so bright that his eyes shut tightly, involuntarily, their remaining sealed until the plane submerged again, into Erie, P.A., where his exile began.

Why he should think of this just now he did not know, but it was ominous.

The right-hand turn signal on N. Emopee's blimp-of-a-station wagon ticked in double time as he pulled from Eunice's house and headed south. Soon the famous Hollywoods, with an "s" on the end, sign in New Burbank was before him, and he felt a great relief. Ah, Hollywoods, where the action was, where wealth, power, and prestige were, where, he continued to feel, his destiny lay. Yes, he did want a fancy title, the right to hobnob with big wigs, ride in limos, and go on hiatus like the best of them. Biz sickness, it was called, but he wanted it, even as, for now, it brought him great despair.

"My bank manager was up here this morning sniffing around, Cleo. He wants to sell this place, wants to cover his loans to me." N. Emopee was back in his wine cellar war room. "You'd better pack your bags."

"Sorry to hear it, Nathan."

"I have had an idea to remedy it, however, to the delight of old Rem I might add, to his dust, and to the remnants of foreign wars. I picked up the idea on television last night, on pubic television, which knows everything about everything. I say I conduct tours here. Income, Cleo, income."

"Really?"

"It's in your best interest too, you know."

"But I'm on Social Security."

"But I let you use my shower."

Cleo saw the point.

N. Emopee marched to his wine bar, two oak casks and a plank of cherry wood, where he poured them both a pommard, not the best of burgundies but nothing a fig newton couldn't make better. "The trick is getting people to come up here, nine out of ten, beyond the city council, having long since forgotten that anyone even lives up here."

"Your odd painter hasn't forgotten."

"What I need, though, is busloads, foreign tourist busloads."

Cleo bounced her bag of bones into the corner and pulled up a bar stool that was taller than she was. "How much of it do you intend to show, Nathan, being the private sort that you are? I mean people are not going to come all the way up here just to look at your red front door."

With a search of the cellar's ceiling, the white-washed beams, and then of the bleached brick walls, N. Emopee reached the unavoidable conclusion. "The whole place, Cleo, the house, the gardens, the grove, everything but this cellar, although I could be persuaded to even open it to tourists."

"How much time do you have before your bank manager brings the locks?"

"Not long, Cleo. The 31st I'd say. The bank manager mumbled something about the 31st."

"That's in three more weeks."

From the latest letters with resume he mailed before the holidays, N. Emopee received two courtesy phone calls, both production companies saying that they would keep his name on file in the event that something suitable came up, making forty Hollywoods filing cabinets he was now in. Even so, he had Emily type several new queries, which he dispatched immediately, arguing to her, "I've got to have letters with resume out at any given moment. There has always got to be hope. I can't wait for OBC." But now even Emily had her doubts.

Which was when he said, "If I don't have a reader job by March 15th, I'm going to drop the whole thing and go back to stage-handing in Pittsburgh." For now, though, he phoned the two story editors from whom he had received courtesy calls, first up a lady at Filmworks. She invited him to return her call if he had any questions regarding her rejection of him, which of course he did.

"I noticed that you've been working for Homer Tank at OBC," the woman, taking the lead, said. "I did too, briefly."

"Mr. Tank has--" N. Emopee, brightly.

"When I was a free-lance analyst years ago, my strategy was to phone story departments around town every other day, a system that worked as long as I didn't become a pain in the butt to them, by my own measure a big pain. Such a plan is not suited to these times, though, too many free-lancers now, companies not taking their calls. What's more, many of the studios and production companies only hire <u>union</u> analysts currently, whom <u>they</u> contact as their needs dictate."

N. Emopee had forgotten that there were union analysts. The lady then invited him to send her a sample of his coverages for her file, closing with, "I wish I could be more encouraging, Mr. Emopee. Have you thought of being a rabbi?"

As for the second call, it was to a story editor at a company called Whirlwind Pictures.

"Hello, is Mr. Ted Deck there?" N. Emopee, firmly.

"Speaking."

"My name is N. Emopee, sir, the N. Emopee whose resume you responded to over the holidays."

"Oh, yes," Deck, in a metallic voice, hoarse, like he'd never spoken to anyone in a month. "To be honest, Emopee, I can't figure out why a fellow with your accomplishments, a globally famous third oboist, would want to work at a story department, this one or any other."

"I can explain it to you, if you have the time," N. Emopee.

"I mean, can you?"

"I'm looking to get in the door is all, after which I hope to move up to other things," like management, if he was lucky, or production.

"I can tell you from my experience, my friend," Deck, going on, "that advancement is not easy in this business under any circumstance, doubly so if you start in a story department."

"Homer Tank at OBC said--"

"I've been in this department for twelve years," bitterness in Deck's voice, followed by, "and it's who you know, all who you know."

Did Deck not know anybody?

"So I've heard," N. Emopee, finally, politely.

"If I were you, I wouldn't get into story analysis but screenwriting. That's where the money is, where the best chance for success is in this business." Both of N. Emopee's screenwriting instructors, Script and Sherm Bird, had said the same thing to him, that analyzing for story departments, which both had done, was a waste of time in the end, most assignments just garbage. Better to be a screenwriter.

"To create my own garbage?"

"Excuse me?" Deck.

In his screenwriting class, though, Bird blasted even screenwriting, because, he said, the odds of making it, so-called, were astronomical.

"But I'm not a screenwriter," N. Emopee back at Deck with certainty, "a story editor like you maybe, a story analyst first and then a story editor, but not a screenwriter."

"It's your choice, Emopee. Just be aware of what you're getting into."

N. Emopee was, would.

"Having said this, I can tell you that Whirlwind is busy just now, so that if you want analysis work, I can give you some. Five feature-length scripts have just come in that need covered."

N. Emopee gasped. "Feature-length, eh?" He hadn't done one of those yet.

"I can pay you $120 a piece for them."

N. Emopee's last coverages were $25 a piece.

"I'll call you on Monday," Deck.

N. Emopee lowered the phone with an excited thump, letting out a whoop as if he'd just won the lottery, which he had in a way, his ticket to full-time bizdom, possibly. As for Deck's pronouncement that advancement was hard to come by for analysts, what about the successes that Tank told him about, readers who were now executives in the industry, and who could all but name their price? Then, again, they were Tank's analysts, not Deck's. He should steer clear of Deck maybe.

Once more that night he paced his apartment, from room to room to balcony to room, stopping from time to time to deliver a soliloquy. Stuck in his mind now, the idea of screenwriting. This was where the money was, where the best chance of success was in the business, at least according to Deck.

"But I can't write for film and TV, can I? Moreover, I don't want to write just for writing's sake, or for women-in-jeopardy movies, for instance, which are hot currently."

He honked once in his handkerchief, capped with a sigh.

"The point is, were I to write a screenplay now, at this stage in my life, I would want it to be meaningful, something worthwhile, from my point of view at least worth doing."

Mr. Deck at Whirlwind Pictures never did phone him back, nor would he return his calls. Why did Deck change his mind? Staring at the next batch of letters with resume, alongside his checklist of all the other Hollywoods executives, agents, editors, department directors, and whoever else he could come up with that he had contacted, N. Emopee felt at last, at long, long last, the futility of it all. Never mind that it was not March 15th yet, not yet his self-imposed deadline for his contingency plans.

But what contingency plans? How serious was he about heading back to Pittsburgh, or doing anything other than big success here in the Woods, in the biz?

His mind returned to Calvin Crump at Popcorn Pictures, for whom he should have unloaded trucks that time, and whose assistant producer position by now would have him where all such assistants went after twelve months. He'd be an associate producer, conceivably, following which the sky was the limit. "I'll be kicking himself for years over this."

He was being hard on himself, naturally, forgetting that he had outgrown truck unloading, and that that assistant producer's job had ulcers written all over it. No, he was an oboist, a third oboist, formerly with the Stiff Arm Symphony, in search of a new line of work, story analyzing for openers, and then maybe story editing, with management a possibility down the road, maybe production. So, it had not panned out for him yet. It still could.

Or it couldn't. As he bumped again onto his balcony, the distant sun collapsing into the river far below, he settled, at last, on pulling the plug on this biz search of his, the wastebasket where his new bunch of letters went, along with the long list of names and addresses that he and Doh had researched so painstakingly. He was tossing in the towel.

His biz search ended? The thought of screenwriting, stuck in N. Emopee's mind for a week now, suddenly blossomed. That's where the big money was and the answer to all of his woes. As for writing something meaningful, something that had something to say, there were lots of screenplays out there that accomplished this. Look at *They Shoot Horses, Don't They?* Why couldn't he do it, too?

Thus he spent the next morning putting furniture, what there was left of it in the house, in his plaid living room. Atmosphere was everything, he recalled from his exile in Erie, where, as a catharsis, he wrote a major short story of sorts, unfortunate and forgettable words, about his West Virginia passport that had been revoked. Any furniture that looked the least bit screenwriterly he, therefore, brought into his living room, now his screenwriting room.

From the second-floor hallway came, to his amazement on finding them still up there, two seven-foot-high book cases, one of which he had made himself from shipping crates, meant as temporary shelving for his texts during his oboe studies. The other one he had salvaged from a trash bin that time he visited Blodgett and Bag at USC, a wide smooth white enamel deal just right for his oversized manuscripts, including his extensive collection of mysticism. From a trash bin? One person's trash was another person's treasure. What people threw out was astounding.

Next, his desk. This would have to be a makeshift one, as his real desk had gone to the electric company to pay his previous month's electric bill. He covered a hollow door from his garage with wood grain contact paper, teak it was, or more likely walnut, which would do just fine, low book cases under either end to hold it up and to hold his telephone answering machine. Over this went a four-foot florescent grow light meant for indoor plants, back when he had indoor plants, before the plant shop took them back to cover their rental bill, but which now flooded the entire surface of his desk. Indeed, it washed the room overall with brilliant light, which, as one who suffered from SAD, seasonal affective disorder, it was paradise.

And last but not least, on a little hook on the side of his desk, a stainless steel miniature oboe that he had been given by the American Oboe Association to mark the two-month anniversary of their blacklisting of him.

Chapter Six
Hick's Used Bookstore

*E*ven though he'd never written one before, albeit he had taken two courses in it, N. Emopee, over the next two days, produced fourteen pages of a screenplay expressing his moral outrage over the latest Hayfields and McCays war, and how this war, indeed how all wars, created an evil far greater than anything they tried to prevent. A second script to follow, if he could get it going, would be on the subject of orphans, an output impressive, in his view, much better than he had expected the first time out. Even so, it was going to take him some time to get used to.

Bothering him now, his painting days, his uncle busy again. Up to then he knew that this necessity might end the very next day, with his new job in the biz. The way it stood for now, however, he would be screenwriting for all the remainder of the year, or longer, depending on his progress, depending on whether he got good enough to make any money at it. The prospect of painting for more than another month, much less for the rest of the year, was depressing to him beyond words.

Then, the pleasure he derived from the writing, when he stopped to consider it further, made it all worthwhile to him, he felt, for however long it lasted. The writing lent him a peace, a serenity, a fulfillment that he had not known since his college days, when, for an elective English class, he wrote a story about a covert operation, led by him, to bring down an invading army. His idea was to use the opponent's own weapons to defeat him, a kind of mass Aikido.

He still had things to work out, the need, for example, for a variety of writing projects underway at one time. The screenwriting was in need of a break now and then, something out in left field where he wasn't restricted by convention. But then, the most difficult adjustment for him was the absence of a major goal, which for the past six months had been his big new job in the biz. Employment in the biz was still his aim, but it would be in a different role this time.

Yet, wasn't writing a screenplay a major goal, and an even greater one than any he'd ever attempted before? Well, yes and no. Yes, in that it obviously was a lot of work, but no, because he was not fully committed to it yet, not quite, for the simple reason that he wasn't sure whether or not he could actually do it. Were he able to get something, anything, produced, or even published for that matter, even an academic journal article, something on Third-Chair oboing, it would make a world of difference to him. At least, in his view, he would be a legitimate writer, have reason to forge ahead.

Stress was also why he was not yet sworn to screenwriting, not for lack of it but for not enough of it. Attempting everything he could think of to get hired in the biz, failing at every turn, then going back for more, he was accustomed to a ton of stress all these months, something he now no longer had. The lack of stress was now stressful for him!

And then there was the house, which his creditors, his father's creditors, to be precise, and the bank, were now dismantling bit by bit, from the top down, with the idea of turning the hill into heaven knew what. He had heard talk of a theme park, of all things. How would Rem feel about that?

At Hick's Used Bookstore that Sunday, N. Emopee discovered Jules crouched under the bulky front counter where he seemed to be petting Bert, except that N. Emopee knew better, knew how Jules hated Bert, and vice versa. Well aware of this, in fact, Mr. Hick rarely scheduled them for the same shift, an inconvenience which had him getting rid of the gnome almost, except that Jules was a tireless worker, was book-knowledgeable, and was good with the customers. They were reasons enough to keep him on for at least a while longer. Besides, Jules had the look that Mr.

Hick, the secret picture painter, liked, where he, Bert, Jules, and Raymond looked right out of a painting by Velasquez.

"Hello, Jules," N. Emopee, kneeing up to the counter.

"Good afternoon, Mr. Emopee," Jules, ratcheting back to his feet.

The conversation usually ended here, Jules not a talker particularly, not an idle chatterer, whereas N. Emopee, after three days of solitary confinement at his screenwriting desk, was up for a word. "Buffing baseboards again, are you?" a broad grin.

Jules, even more humorless than usual, "We have no baseboards here," pointing out where they would be if they had them.

N. Emopee looked for himself, being polite, and then said, to undo it, "Right you are, Jules."

As one who merely reacted to others, never initiated anything if he could help it, characteristic of everyone N. Emopee had ever known, now that he thought about it, Jules waited to see what N. Emopee had to say to him next.

"Did any mysticism come in this week?" N. Emopee, at last.

His vast black moustache getting a massage, Jules reviewed in his mind the cartons of books that Mr. Hick had purchased over the past seven days, while N. Emopee, recalling that Jules also had an appetite for the subject, was poised to doubt his answer, his opening answer anyway.

"No," the clerk, in the end; "no mysticism."

Which meant that they may or may not have had some come in. "Are you sure?" N. Emopee. "Are you completely sure?"

N. Emopee studied Jules, who considered it a second further, and, by the look of him, another time on top of that.

For a small guy, this Jules certainly had a lot of hair on him, it occurred to N. Emopee as he watched him. In addition to his moustache he had thick black hair from his biceps to his finger tips, hair crawling from the top of his shirt, as though trying to get out, hair above his eyes, less eyebrows than hedgerows, and even hair spilling from his ears. A bear he was to see him. N. Emopee's perusal of him had the usually unflappable Jules all on edge all of a sudden, prompting him to reveal, in a sudden stutter, "When you came in I was going through a box of books that Mr. Hick bought just last night, so there might be something for you in there that I haven't come to yet."

"If not mysticism, then screenplays, perhaps. Any screenplays?"

Jules leaned over and hoisted the banged-up box onto the counter, the contents of which he tumbled out onto the counter with a loud thump. "Help yourself," he said.

N. Emopee grinned, awkwardly, not sure whether this was done in anger or just in haste. He'd have a look just the same.

"You are an actor aren't you, Jules?" N. Emopee in the meantime. "Didn't I hear you say once that you are an actor?"

Flattered, his buttons pushed, or one of them at least, Jules started out. "My most challenging role was that of the troubled youth Alan Strang in Peter Shaffer's play '*Equus*,' which I performed in a regional theatre in Ohio, in the Cleveland Regional Theatre, no less."

"Cleveland, eh?" acknowledged N. Emopee. "But now why was it such a challenging part for you?"

Jules, taking a breath, then bending forward, "If you know the story at all, Alan blinded six horses."

N. Emopee pulled back. "You don't say."

A shrug, Jules, "Trust me."

"And so as an actor you had to find this in yourself, huh, had to find something in you that would do such a thing, I mean to make it believable?"

"I had to do this, yes."

N. Emopee, his eyes narrowing, "So did you find it?"

"That's why I'm a clerk in a used bookstore." Jules twirled his finger at the side of his head indicating insanity.

N. Emopee, "Oh, my," the best he could do.

"And how about you?" Jules anxious to change the subject. "Are you an actor, too? You seem to know something about it?"

"Not an actor, although I took a drama class one time."

"A class?"

"It was quite good on the human condition, that class, the closer to the bone the better." N. Emopee was himself suddenly passionate.

Jules swigged from a can of soda on the edge of the front counter.

"Modern allegory, like Beckett."

Jules sank a second gulp of soda.

"Desperate humor, like Ionesco."

With a third slug of soda, Jules looked ready to fizz over, leaving N. Emopee to leave it at that. At the same time he rather expected Jules to ask him, hoped he would say to him, "If you're not an actor, then what are you? What do you do?"

Now, four days back N. Emopee would have dreaded this, would have hated having to explain, once again, how he was an oboist, but an oboist unemployed at the moment, probably forever, and that consequently he was attempting to find employment in the Woods, in some capacity in the Woods, but that it wasn't going well, not well at all just then. This time, though, he would allow as how he was a screenwriter, even though he was a screenwriter only kind of, not fully committed to it yet, definitely not produced yet, but a screenwriter just the same.

Yet, sadly enough, no such question came from Jules, who ambled down to the rest room, "Le Cannes," as Mr. Hick had it on the sign on the door, N. Emopee remaining in place, if only for a moment, to try "screenwriter" out. He would test it to see how it sounded, in case the opportunity came to him the next time. "I'm a writer, a screenwriter," quietly out loud, a daring declaration at that. He glanced over his shoulder to make sure no one had heard him.

Remaining, however, were the books Jules had dumped onto the counter. He must not leave until he took a look. It turned out that there was nothing there that was up his alley, not even *Zipper Issues*, a book of erotica. He'd never seen erotica at Hick's. Then he never looked for it either.

As for mysticism, it didn't appear promising--until the very bottom of the pile, where he came upon spiritual teacher Ram Dass' autobiography *Be Here Now*. He had read it years ago, and while it wasn't mysticism per se, it did contain mystical moments. For instance there was when Ram Dass, not yet Ram Dass but Professor Richard Alpert, met, for the first time, his guru to be, Neem Karoli Baba. Neem Karoli Baba said something to him that startled him, the line in the book escaping him over the decades. He would take a quick look to see if he could spot it.

Instantly almost, there it was, jumping out at him. Neem Karoli Baba said "Haven't we met before?" the implication being that in the spiritual world they knew each other once upon a time. The further suggestion was that Neem Karoli Baba still had one foot in the spiritual world, carrying with him a spiritual memory.

But now Jules was back again. "Is there anything more I can help you with, Mr. Emopee?"

N. Emopee was without words, but then said, "No, you've helped me quite enough for today, Jules."

One thought, however, N. Emopee couldn't get out of his mind. How did the producers at Popcorn and Famous Films come to say the line to him, on what authority, and what about the brochure stuck in his door that had "Haven't we met before?" written on it, along with his name? What was the connection?

N. Emopee insisted on not being a conventional screenwriter, on not writing screenplays just for sake of writing screenplays, in service of the latest hot topic, yet how could he make money at it otherwise? Sure, there were unconventional screenwriters who were successful regardless. Look at Fellini. However, weren't they the exception, radical writers who could write anything and succeed at it?

This proved to be the least of N. Emopee's problems, for the next morning he found that his screenplay-in-progress concerning his opposition to the latest West Virginia war back in the day, he no longer liked, didn't like the feel of it, meddling with emotions too real and too important to him to treat in such an offhanded manner.

Next, his academic journal article on Third-Chair oboing ceased to interest him, teaching the way it felt, and he wanted nothing to do with teaching. His father taught for a time, before he died of it, and he didn't want to be like his father, death aside. That his father was not a father to him than a visiting professor was what that was all about, that resentment.

As for writing something out in left field, he couldn't get out of center field now for some reason, his ideas as compelling as cement. It took ten years to learn how to write, the word was, and here he'd fallen apart in the first week.

In his dim, plaid living room he dropped onto his oriental chair beside a carved figure of the bodhisattva Avalokitesvara, across from which was his screenwriting desk, abandoned now, his exile in Erie all over again, Erie where he wrote his first little story, that regrettable, forgettable small tale about his West Virginia passport.

Striving like this, as Ed his Buddhist painter always put it, wanting things, trying to do this or to be that, was the source, exactly, of so much suffering in the world. Certainly it was responsible for N. Emopee's misery just then. The past six months had unquestionably been painful for him, attempting first to get back into show business, as a reader for openers, and then as a story editor hopefully, and finally as a manager of some kind, possibly even an executive, a CEO, Chief Executive Oboist, and now taking on this screenwriting monster, just because it was where the money was, well, he had to be out of his mind.

He stared at his calendar, at the bright red circle around the 30th . This was his latest deadline and the date by which he must have one of his screenwriting projects completed, and produced, or he'd drop the whole thing. But hadn't he dropped it already, just now dropped it?

N. Emopee had never shown One Pound Down Street to a living soul, not even to Cleo, who knew it only as the downstairs shower, and who, understandably, was now all eyes. N. Emopee was conducting tours through the entire place, and so it was that here again this day Cleo, as his assistant, donned her best crow feather frock, her plumage pullover, and off they went.

Off they went but not without the inevitable first question, "Where does the name One Pound Down Street come from?" not an unreasonable query, but one leaving N. Emopee searching for words. Finally, "a local writer came up with it." This was how he understood it, he said, from what he had heard. "He was on a diet," a chuckle from someone on a diet, too. He'd like to have said that Rem came up with the name, but Rem had never been on a diet in his life.

"Here you see the Emopee organ," not needing clarification but getting one anyway from N. Emopee, "the musical instrument that is," another chortle from the audience. No one was more startled to have come upon it than N. Emopee himself. He'd forgotten about it there in an alcove on the second floor.

"What's this?" someone asked too late, for down the lever came. And with it a great roar from below, a rumble from under the floor, as the bellows in the bowels of the building inhaled, only to exhale soon after. The instrument came fully, if not fiercely, to life. As it happened this same person knew the "Jelly Roll Rag" and with a tickle of the tiles had everyone, including Cleo, rocking in the hall.

The dining room, as Cleo pointed out to another group later in the day, was in the shape of an oval, an elongated ethereal blue oval with a table for ten shaped exactly the same.

"This is all well and good," Cleo, with a dramatic wave, "but in practical terms, it's a disaster." It was remarkable how bold Cleo had become in this role. "You see, those sitting at either end of the table, N. Emopee himself at the north end, have no place to rest their elbows.   As one without elbows this is not a problem for N. Emopee, but for the guest at the south end, the guest of honor, who had elbows in abundance, typically, it couldn't be worse." Cleo demonstrated, her elbows slipping off the table.

This group understood few words of this, regrettably, a language barrier, but the demonstration part they did pick up on, and they laughed raucously.

To see Rufus and N. Emopee together left no doubt that they were relatives. They could pass for brothers. Rufus sometimes pointed this out, in a joking manner, to his customers, a way in which he could be perfectly charming. No doubt this was partly why his painting business flourished over the years. "We're brothers," he would say, despite their thirty-year age difference, and his customers would always smile.

The trouble was, having built his business Rufus had become bound to it. He couldn't get out from under it if he wanted to. He couldn't collect social security without it, for instance, funds he feared the government would run out of before he got his share. Didn't he say it to N. Emopee over and over? To put it another way, no one was more a slave to the "almighty dollar," as he called it, than he was, even though, for the sake of his health, he'd be better off free of it.

It was said that if a child was offered a nickel now or a quarter later, the child would take the nickel now. So it was with Rufus. Once he'd finished a job, he wanted to be paid for it on the spot, now not later. Then when he got the money, there was no putting it away for a rainy day. Today was the rainy day. Trips to Hawaii and England were how he spent it.

Regarding his passion for travel, this came from his father, who was a painter too. Otto, while he loved trains, planes, and automobiles, as it were, traveled rarely, for the simple reason that he couldn't afford it, but he did on occasion get away. Rufus couldn't swing it either, really, but he surely tried. And he couldn't for the life of him figure out why N. Emopee wasn't just as keen on it as he was. He had it all figured out how. N. Emopee could ride throughout Europe on a Europass, staying in hostels at night, and eating vegetables from the countryside.

Wonderful for Rufus but not good for N. Emopee was that N. Emopee drove himself just as hard at painting as he did at screenwriting. Where other uncles might be worried about a nephew wound tighter than a drum, Rufus knew a good thing when he saw it, and so he pushed him even harder.

While on the phone at the end of the month with adopted Eunice, N. Emopee did not mention his screenwriting, nor did Eunice ask him what he was doing these days. She knew, at least, that it was not oboing anymore with the Stiff Arm Symphony, fortunately in her opinion not oboing, as she who hated oboe music, but it wasn't teaching either, unfortunately in her view. She loved teaching, and teachers. She married N. Emopee's dad, after all, who was teaching at that time. His turning to screenwriting would represent yet another step in the wrong direction. This left his adopted sister April as the sole subject of their conversation, or of Eunice's conversation anyway, how April's third marriage the previous year, to her latest boy friend Skippy, was such a blessing. Weren't they expecting a child, Skippy the third, late that summer.

And wasn't Skippy senior the clever one, she proclaimed. The driver of a potato chip truck during the day, he was an inventor by night. His latest creation was artificial seaweed. "You have to SEA it to believe it," was his slogan, even though he didn't know yet what artificial seaweed was good for. Christmas tree tinsel was a possibility.

N. Emopee was interested in all of this, sort of, but not very, because he knew that this was his mother making him feel guilty once more. She also made him feel guilty over his on-going bachelorhood, a choice he soliloquized about quite often at his house, and quite to the point.

"Affairs of the heart are not the source of happiness, not a true and reliable source of happiness. This is because all is transient, changing, ever changing, where nothing is today what it was yesterday, and nothing will be tomorrow what it is today. Today's lover is tomorrow's stranger. Take April, divorced three times now."

Hieronymus Hup, the conductor of the Stiff Arm Symphony, had a thing for oboes. This explained why his orchestra was made up entirely of oboes at one point, one hundred and thirty-two of them, what became one hundred and thirty-three when N. Emopee signed up. The one exception was the one French Horn out on the end of the fourth row, which Hup meant as an exclamation point.

N. Emopee was Third Oboist, a Third Oboist not the Third Oboist, one of three, designated by letters, Third Oboist (a), Third Oboist (b), Third Oboist (c). He was (c). Then again, he was the only one of the group with a national reputation, so there was that.

It was this very notoriety that had him thinking that old Hup might yet give him part-time oboing work. It would be just for old time's sake, N. Emopee would say, fifty bucks a pop to keep the lights on at his house one more day, particularly as the auctioning of his wine collection yielded him only a fraction of what he had anticipated. There was more of his homemade pomegranate port in there than he realized, an acquired taste he was the first to admit, even for an alcoholic like himself.

Unfortunately, Hup, a German from the Black Forest, had a guttural R in his speech, the rattle of which was like listening to a locomotive on a bad track. Thus, "Afterrr all these months away from oboing, Heirrr Emopee, you'd have to starrrt all overrr again, starrrt, in your case, at one hundrrred and thirty-second chair, an interrrrnship that wouldn't buy you the time of day."

Hup's feelings had been hurt, as had been the feelings of the American Oboe Association, regarding his, N. Emopee's, outlandish attempt at alternative oboing, a job in the biz, in other words, as if conventional oboing was not worth the pucker producing it. Accordingly, it would take N. Emopee a decade, give or take a year, to work his way all the way back up to Third Oboist (c), making the effort, in practical terms, undoable, unoboible.

But what about playing for another symphony, this being West Virginia, the oboe capital of the world, lots of organizations for him to play for around the state. Why not, for example, go back to the Embouchure Ensemble across the river in Westhill?

Heir Hup summed up the bad news to him this way: "The worrrd is out on you, N. Emopee. No one that I know of would be willing to risk your corrrrrupting influence. Conforrrmity, conforrrmity, conforrrrrrmity, is the name of the game in oboing, as the brrrotherrrhood of oboists knows too well, as you know too, or once knew, before you chose to be differrrent."

N. Emopee, a defiant frown. "My eyesight is good now," he tried, even though it wasn't.

"Besides," Hup concluding, "you've an arrrthritic left rrring fingerrr, I noticed, a new development forrr you, joining yourrr dad and Samuel Beckett, so you arrre shorrrt a note, arrren't you? That's the last thing I, or any otherrr orchestrrra needs these days, the demanding earrrs that we play forrr. By coming to me like this, you'rrre just being desperrrate."

Where had N. Emopee heard that before?

"Buddhism teaches that the individual determines what happens to him." This was Ed the painter. "The individual, not something 'out there,' is responsible for his fate. The external world only reacts to what the individual does."

"The bending of my left ring finger is not something I did, but the external world is certainly reacting to it."

"If *you* didn't bend your finger, then who did?"

In the course of moving drop sheets and ladders while painting houses, N. Emopee was aware that an abundance of creatures, snails, butterflies, spiders, moths, and bees, were crushed, smashed, or smothered. "Start the day with a little death," he said all the time, said sadly. But it raised with him the Buddhist issue of ahimsa, the principle of non-injury to other creatures, respect for all living things, to put it another way, where monks in India carried staffs as they walked through the woods, tapping ahead of them to ward off animals and insects, lest by accident they should get trampled.

Now, N. Emopee was not a monk, or not one yet, but he chose to practice ahimsa all the same, as he did variously in Pittsburgh, and again here in the Woods, including at One Pound Down Street. There, uninvited critters were not put to death for being themselves, but were scooped up and deposited back outside instead. That ahimsa would be a point of conflict between his uncle and him was inevitable, and thus was the case when they came upon a colony of wasps high in the eaves of a house they were painting just north of town. N. Emopee, as atonement for all those that he had destroyed in his past lives, or so he decided, refused to do in this lot. "My personal philosophy," he told Rufus, to the point.

Thinking it a joke, Rufus laughed once, then handed N. Emopee an aerosol can of black paint, being out of his bug spray, to squirt on the wasps. "Be a man," he said.

"My manhood has nothing to do with it," N. Emopee, declining the container. "It's the principle of ahimsa."

Rufus, flustered now, argued that it was the junior man's responsibility to clear away all pests on the job and that if N. Emopee wasn't prepared to do so, then there were lots of other painters out there who were. N. Emopee held his ground, though, with, "Forget it." Was he being unreasonable? Was the damnation of his immortal soul at stake here, really?

"We'll split it then," Rufus, impatiently. "You start, I'll finish."

N. Emopee just stood there, his job in jeopardy now, a question of who this meant more to, even as Rufus saw it now as a who's-the-boss contest.

The next hour was a standoff, the two of them avoiding the wasps, until, at last, it was the only section on the house left to be painted--before Rufus got paid.

Well, while N. Emopee was away at lunch the wasps did get a paint job, a spraying which, according to the homeowner next door, was a comedy the likes of which he'd never seen before. Rufus, a marionette on a string to see him, leaped around, squirting and retreating, squirting and retreating, until it was clear that what this was truly all about was Rufus' mortal fear of wasps.

To N. Emopee the question was then, what else was his uncle afraid of that would cause them conflict? No, the sooner he could make money from his screenwriting and be done with painting, the better for everybody.

Chapter Seven
Encounter with Professor
Blodgett

*W*ith all the pacing and soliloquies in his apartment N. Emopee had worn quite a track in his old carpet. The blue had turned gray. Yet it was not for naught, because his marching up and down had yielded the connection between the two producers and the mysterious brochure stuck in his door. He saw now that he was the common denominator; he himself had caused the three. A spiritual something in him had caused them. The question "Haven't I seen you before?" would not have happened except that he prompted it.

But what did this mean? It meant that something spiritual in him was asking him this question.

N. Emopee remained in a precarious state, psychologically. Aware that Eunice was giving him the cold shoulder, he mailed her the artist's journal he had been keeping, excerpts from it anyway, hoping that she would better understand what he was doing, and why he was doing it, even though he wasn't sure himself any longer.

His mother's reaction to the passages, when at last she received them, was to feel flattered, in a way, that he would share something so personal with her, and embarrassed, in another, for the same reason. She said as much the next time he phoned her, where she avoided, in quite the balancing act, talking in any detail about it. She wound up talking once more about April and Skippy. "The ultrasound shows clearly now that it is not another Skippy, a Skippy junior, that they are having this summer, but a Skippi. And she's going to be a big one."

And so it went for another week. To his credit, N. Emopee did complete one of his projects, as per his ultimatum, and his latest 30th deadline, something "out in left field," even though in his estimation it was neither producible nor publishable. It was too, well, mystical.

He wrote in his journal,

Regarding the story I've just written, I feel 'called.' I have begun to 'know,' at last. I deem it is mystical, mystical in the sense of mystery, but what is the feeling exactly? Of being attuned, of being aligned in a Taoist way, to where I feel as if I've been adrift for all these years, but have suddenly, in my groping in the river, latched onto a log, the log, which is racing steadily and surely toward my destiny. All the while I do not know the nature of this log, nor that of the steady current in which we now so effortlessly flow. Nor do I know to where precisely we are rushing. I do not fear it, though, wishing only to go with it, toward its, our, intended completion.

Well, this was all well and good except that it wasn't paying his bills, he reminded himself. The water company couldn't care less about his intended completion.

The following week N. Emopee was again on the campus of USC in the Woods, this time to retrieve five audio tapes from Professor Blodgett, recorded translations of Dvorak's oboe music, not previously rendered from the Czech into English, quite a different sound, tapes which he paid a graduate student in the Czechoslovakian Music department to prepare for him and which Blodgett wanted to dub for his own purposes, if N. Emopee was willing to lend them to him.

Aware that the loaned tapes were with Blodgett's secretary, N. Emopee decided to not look in on his former mentor, mainly due to the catastrophe of their last meeting, that fiasco at the campus restaurant. However, when he slipped into the secretary's office, she informed him that the professor was at his desk just then, that if N. Emopee cared to say hello to him he was welcome to do so.

Of course, N. Emopee could <u>not</u> now go in. What if the secretary told Blodgett that his former favorite student was there, ten feet away, but chose to avoid him?

Thus, "Come," came the familiar grainy voice following two raps on his door.

N. Emopee breathed a breath, adjusted his coke-bottle glasses, then slowly stepped in.

Dug in at his desk, a frown at his brow, and with a short cigarette smoldering in his long right hand, Blodgett was sifting through a stack of scholarly music, by the look of him, or was it department business now that he was chair, chair of the Comparative Oboing Department?

"I've caught you at a bad time again, professor," N. Emopee, his hands suddenly in his pockets. "Another day perhaps, huh?"

"No, no, N.," Blodgett, not looking up. "Don't be silly."

Firmly into the office now, no turning back, N. Emopee clicked closed the door behind him, just as the professor, his blood-streaked eyes raising, gestured for him to take the couch opposite him. His cigarette flared with the poke. N. Emopee's eyes leaped at the burst of fire prompting Blodgett to stub the cigarette out, abruptly, in the ashtray beside him.

"It's just that I've never seen you smoke before," N. Emopee, awkwardly.

"No, I don't suppose you have, have you?"

"You told us that you were a three-pack-a-day man, until you quit with the help of acupuncture."

Which left the professor to shrug, solemnly, "Chairing the department has started it up again, I'm sorry to say, I regret to admit to you. Now all the needles in China couldn't--"

N. Emopee frowned, but then, "I just stopped by to pick up those Dvorak tapes I loaned you last year, if you've dubbed them for yourself at this point."

"I had a work-study student do it, yes, a big job."

"Thanks for letting me retrieve them," N. Emopee, after a long pause.

Blodgett stared.

"You see, I have an academic journal article I need them for," a lie the minute it left his lips. The real reason was, the longer the professor had them the more he would conclude that N. Emopee didn't want them any longer. The professor would think that they belonged to <u>him</u> now, if he hadn't decided this already. In fact, N. Emopee <u>did</u> sort of want them for that academic piece even though his writing it any time soon was doubtful.

Another awkward silence followed while N. Emopee waited for Blodgett to reciprocate the thank you, inasmuch as he, N. Emopee, had loaned him translations that had cost him $250 to have prepared, a fortune to him at the time. No return thank you came, though, leaving N. Emopee to wonder whether, according to some academic protocol, such tapes were expected to be donated to the professor guiding a student's studies.

Yet, it was over now anyway, was it not, to where he crawled to his feet to leave. Especially he wanted to get out of there before the subject of his career came up, as surely it would the longer he remained there, remembering that his lunch with Blodgett was all about his becoming a teacher. That seemed eons ago. Then again, in a subsequent phone call, he did reveal to Blodgett that he had become a reader at OBC television, which, the way it was going, he no longer was either.

But alas it was too late. "I take it that you're not looking for a teaching job anymore," the OBC work getting no mention at all, as if it didn't count. Blodgett's murky eyes hovered over the top of his half glasses, half down.

In a sober, genuine, more animated than usual manner then, N. Emopee let fly with what he was certain would be a revelation not the least bit convincing, but which he felt compelled to attempt all the same. "Something unexpected has happened to me," he began surely but unsteadily.

With a brush back of his bushy gray hair, the front part of it in particular, which N. Emopee had long admired because it made him, the professor, look like a writer, Blodgett smiled, then grinned a grin of seeming bemusement.

"You see," N. Emopee went on, "in my younger years I was a would-be writer, philosophical and political pieces for the most part, most of which were regrettable and forgettable, but I always hoped to one day to have another shot at. As luck, bad luck, would have it, the opportunity never came. Until now that is."

Blodgett's eyes brightened, just as N. Emopee's dimmed.

"You may as well know that I am writing screenplays these days. I work in a trade part-time and that allows me the majority of my week for screenwriting."

Blodgett wanted to hear more about it, by the look of him, his eyebrows high.

"In fact," N. Emopee, encouraged by this, "I noted to myself on the way down here, how previously it had bothered me, embarrassed me even, that I did not have a teaching position like you have. Now, if I may say so, not having one is a source of great joy to me. It is a relief, you might say. I feel liberated. My days, my writing days, are filled with existential moments, to use your term for it, instances when I feel more alive and in control of my life than at any other time I can remember."

N. Emopee watched as Blodgett tilted back in his chair, a large green mint into his leathery cheek.

"I should tell you, too," N. Emopee, summing up with a breath, "that with the life experiences I've gained recently, particularly as a Third-Chair oboist with the Stiff Arm Symphony, and with the artistic maturity I realized from your program here at the university, my screenwriting is far richer than I ever imagined it could be, to the extent that I'll complete a full-length film by the end of the year."

Blodgett crunched down on his mint.

"Anyway, I won't take any more of your time, professor. I know how valuable it is," whereupon he was up and on his way to the door.

"This is good, N." the professor, after him, "very good. I must say, though, you certainly are full of surprises." On the professor's face, suddenly, was an expression of knowing exactly what this was all about, as if he, Blodgett, was a writer himself at one time, a screenwriter or maybe a novelist, or still wanted to be. Indeed, "I look forward to the day when I am free of all this stuff," a wave of his hand over the papers on his desk, "so I too--"

Just then the secretary leaned into the room to tell him that he was late for his three o'clock lecture, prompting Blodgett's, "You see what I mean?"

Back at the parking structure N. Emopee unlocked his car door for the twenty-minute race back to his house, where he sighed as deeply as he had all day long. The unexpected support of his mentor had been a lift for him, no question about it, while he noted at the same time how he had pulled off one of the better acting jobs of his life. He could thank, again, that drama class he took that time. Because the fact remained that he did not know whether he was a screenwriter or not, whether he should be one, wanted to be one, or whether he shouldn't go back to Pittsburgh and become a stagehand once more, or maybe a plumber.

When asked by friends what her son was doing these days, N. Emopee's adopted mother insisted on saying that he was painting houses with her brother, not a single mention of screenwriting. When N. Emopee learned of it, it infuriated him, made him feel miserable all over again. Also painful, his suspected loss of credibility with his former stagehanding boss, his hero, at the RBC staging department back in Pittsburgh, to whom, when he left RBC to return to West Virginia, he promised great success. And his boss believed him. Why shouldn't he? And, sure enough, didn't he earn a B.O. degree, Bachelor of Oboing, and then a position with the world-renowned, well, the state-renowned Stiff Arm Symphony there in Morganhill?

But with his release from the symphony, due to his failing eyesight, and more recently because of that arthritic left ring finger, F-sharp, and his subsequent failure to land a permanent alternative oboing job, story analyzing in the biz, N. Emopee was faced now with persuading his boss that <u>this</u> time he <u>would</u> succeed. This was even though the likelihood of his achieving success as a screenwriter was less than his succeeding as a reader, had he even been able to get hired as one.

But then, all of a sudden, a reply to a letter with resume that he had sent out two months prior. The executive vice president of Pictures Corporation informed him that they anticipated new alternative oboe positions, corporate oboing, in the near future, and that they would contact him when they were ready to do an interview. "Just what I need," N. Emopee, his arms in the air. "Settled on a shot at screenwriting, everything explained to everyone, myself included, suddenly the possibility of THE JOB."

As second floors went, N. Emopee's at the house was nothing to sneeze at, even though it was fully exposed now thanks to his scavenger creditors. Among the rooms whistling in the wind, his wax museum, where he had full-size likenesses of historic oboes on display. These ranged from sixteenth century waits, shawms, and bumbardes, all the way up to the Emopeeoboe, his own creation obviously, with its innovative ninth hole, a note without a name. Three centuries of oboe development were recorded in wax for all of heaven to see now, until, that is, he moved them downstairs to his study at the last minute.

Also on the second floor was his ballroom, with its voluptuous views, three-hundred-and-sixty-degree vistas, first of Morganhill down to the east, then of the pomegranate grove to the south, with its rookery large and lively. To the west was the Missing River, when it wasn't missing, and to the north, the white cliffs of White Cliffs, scenes all visible from the vast glass windows and balcony that lined the house midway up the oak siding.

But alas, a message to him on his answering machine from his bank confirmed that all this would be gone soon, too. It was to make way for that theme park that had been rumored, Mickey Mountain. The message also said that the lawyer, Nestor Hestormantle, whom N. Emopee had retained to retain the house did not have a leg, much less, before long, a balcony, to stand on. "Have a nice day."

In all his dejection, N. Emopee decided that the time had come for him to phone his adopted big sister in Pittsburgh, worried as he was that April, having not heard from him for, what was it now, six years, might get the wrong impression. She might think that he was mad at her, when he was only mad at himself. The same worry was on April's mind, he supposed, knowing her as well as he did, in the past at least, to the extent that their calls would collide midway in the wire.

He raised the receiver with a noticeable pa-plick.

If their relationship was at all on shaky ground, he thought to himself pausing for a moment, it was over their reasons, all those years ago, for leaving West Virginia. To hear April tell it they were identical, expulsion from the state over their opposition to the latest Hayfields and McCays war, when nothing could be further from the truth. She, unlike him, had not been tossed out of the state by both the Hayfields and McCays, to say nothing of the State court, but instead had left on her own, for her own reasons.

Then, surely this was a misunderstanding on his part, his sister not so dishonest as to misrepresent herself this way. Giving her the benefit of the doubt was the best idea, remembering how she had given him the same when he became a stagehand and then a plumber. And she otherwise was generous to him, when, for instance, she phoned to congratulate him on his completing his B.O. degree.

Now there was another thing, as down came the receiver with a bump. Despite enough course credits for two degrees, the problem with switching majors too often, April had not finished her college work until years later, until Pittsburgh. It was in Pittsburgh that she completed her degree in education, making her, at last, a credentialed high school biology teacher. But it was in the same semester as N. Emopee earned his B.O. degree, stealing his thunder in effect. Didn't their parents think how splendid it was that she was a certified teacher finally, while not mentioning at all <u>his</u> no-small accomplishment, a Bachelor of Oboing degree?

On the other hand, maybe April wanted only to prove that she was just as worthy, for lack of a better word, as N. Emopee, that she was not, how do you say, chopped liver, that she was deserving of respect in her own right. She'd earned that respect. He quickly raised the receiver again.

"Yes, but April never did anything on her own initiative in her whole life," N. Emopee in a lather, all of a sudden. "Monkey-see monkey-do is what it's been from day one. She always does what I do." The receiver back down with a bang.

Then again, imitation was the sincerest form of flattery was it not, or the <u>severest</u> form of flattery to use his own expression for it? He hiked the receiver back to his ear.

Why, though, since her call to him six years earlier, hadn't she been in touch with him either, not even a letter? Or was it his turn now, April waiting for him to reciprocate in one way or another?

Then, again, the prospect of his asking her for money to save the house, which he would never do, stood in her way, possibly. She didn't want to turn him down, which she most certainly would.

"Hello, April?"

"Hello, N."

As it turned out, this was the high point of their conversation, neither having much to say in the end. N. Emopee in particular was wordless, having accomplished nothing of late, in either his bid for a job in the biz, as a reader to begin with, and then as an editor, and finally as a manager, if all went well for him, or, most recently, in his attempt at screenwriting. The result was that he wound up asking her a lot of questions, just to have something to say. A police interrogator was what he sounded like, keeping April off balance, so that <u>she</u> asked <u>him</u> a lot of questions in return, monkey-see monkey-do, only questions, it was pathetic.

The full-length film that N. Emopee alluded to in his speech to Blodgett did not begin in earnest for another two days. This was the attempt that, should he prove unsuccessful, would mean the demise of "N. Emopee, screenwriter," the collapse of that house of cards, including the end of N. Emopee himself, most probably, hadn't he become suicidal?

Then there was the house painting with Rufus, where if he didn't have a productive three days of screenwriting, the painting days were like hell for him, to where he felt like only a painter. Downtime was also a problem. His nonstop writing and painting did not allow him time to relax, give him a chance to recharge his batteries, which as the weeks passed revealed itself in a hard brow, sunken eyes, and short temper.

That his uncle was concerned about this at least one time was doubtless to his credit, didn't he suggest that N. Emopee take a day off. "Take some time to play, have fun," he put it. It must not, though, be one of the painting days, to which N. Emopee replied, cavalierly, that his writing was his fun, his play, even though it wasn't. In fact, screenwriting was harder work than house painting could ever be, and that was saying a lot.

Mainly, though, he did not want his uncle to suspect that he was having second thoughts about his new career, or that he was failing at his full-length film, which he was just then. His not succeeding was because he had never written a full-length film before, a case of his not knowing what he was doing, and he was not about to admit this to his uncle.

"Why can't they just give me the money?" he laughed to his uncle, only to realize that this was what Rufus himself said all the time regarding his painting customers, which depressed him even more.

N. Emopee was not known to pray much, despite feeling spirituality in his heart. Suddenly, though, he could avoid it no longer, for his sanity. The first words from his lips, however, or rather the first words he was about to say, raised the hair on the back of his neck. It was as though he'd stepped off a cliff. He gasped loudly and nearly fainted. A channel had opened in him, and it scared him half to death.

Cleo had been noticeably scarce of late, so much so that N. Emopee worried that she had packed it in. Didn't she say she felt like her life was winding down? "Heaven help her," N. Emopee, as down over the hill he dove. Into the pomegranate grove, under the raucous rookery, he dashed into Cleo's camp. There, as it turned out, the only trace of her was her TV tray that held a half-eaten wild mushroom omelet with tartar sauce, and a chocolate cookie.

Wild mushroom? But mushrooms on this hill were poisonous. Wasn't it the fate of more than one marauding opossum? Others of them were hallucinogenic, the misfortune of his cat Louise who, as a result, smiled herself to death, and of Helmut his schnauzer, who believed the letter carrier was his Puppy Chow. N. Emopee was frantic now.

His war room wine cellar was the first possibility, so he raced back up the hill to the stone stairs behind which was the dark, damp, door to the cellar. With a hard shove he opened it, but, alas, no Cleo there either. All he found was empty shelves and discarded chits from the previous week's auction of all his wine.

"Cleo?" N. Emopee, calling all the same.

"Cleo?" an echo came back.

Maybe the Missing River was where she went, whether she wanted to or not, in search of the perfect crow bone, possibly, her preoccupation of the past year. All he had to do was find the river, which he hadn't been able to do in his last five attempts.

Nonetheless, he dragged himself all the way down the hill, to the footpath where once there was a sign that read THIS WAY TO THE MISSING RIVER, except that the sign was missing now, too. Barber-pole fashion then, he wound on down, until, after wading through a patch of juniper bushes that he had meant to remove the previous spring, he toppled into the currently currentless concrete runoff canal beside the Morganhill freeway. "Ah, the Missing River!" he cried out.

But then, "Cleo, what on earth are you doing down here?" Cleo was scrambling up the opposite bank for the freeway. Her thumb was out, even though hitch-hiking on the freeway was illegal.

Just then an MHP, a Morganhill Highway Patrol, car pulled over to see what was the matter here, to make an arrest, if need be, or to issue a citation. "What's this all about, folks?" N. Emopee was able to get across the dry riverbed and up the embankment quickly.

"Cleo here has run away," N. Emopee to the officer, hysterically.

"Is this so, madame?" It was the first time in her life Cleo had ever been called "madame" so she just grinned.

"No, officer," she said at last.

"No?" the officer.

"No?" N. Emopee.

Cleo pulled herself up straight. "You see, I'm pregnant. I'm going to the hospital to have my baby."

Cleo was an old woman, so, of course, the suspicions of the policeman were raised.

"Chocolate cookies it sounds like to me," he said finally.

Chapter Eight
It Will Pass

N. Emopee swayed before a crowd of climbers from the local Sierra Club, who had clawed up the hill for a closer look at the pomegranate grove. Pomegranate trees were unheard of this far north, heard of now, though, thanks to N. Emopee's ad in the local paper for his tours. Anyone willing to spend a buck could get a sample of the full tour, including the whole pomegranate grove, by turning up in the grove at 9:00 a.m. on Saturday mornings. Yet, if it was pomegranates that this group wanted to hear about, it was not what they got.

"The oboe," N. Emopee set out, "was invented by a hippie in Pittsburgh in 1968. This individual lived in the suburb of Hautbois, pronounced 'oboe,' in a rented house with a collection of like-minded artisans. Leather sandals, candles, and musical instruments were their specialties. Their oboe, in fact, began as a candle."

Raised eyebrows.

"A man of many interests, a hippy for all seasons, this person also cultivated strawberries in his spare time, paramount among them the now famous Hautbois, again pronounced 'oboe,' strawberry, Fragaria moschata, to where during summers, street vendors in the farmer's market down at the riverfront could be heard calling out 'Fine ripe oboes!'

A short laugh, and a ripple of applause from the climbers, who had never heard such baloney, but who were caught up in it now. They drew closer.

"Most remarkable about this new instrument was that it could be played with either a double reed or a metal mouth piece like a trumpet, versatility if ever there was, which allowed the musician to play in either the woodwind or the brass section, depending upon who called in sick that day."

This was hilarious. Everyone looked at each other.

"There were folks, though, who didn't care for this new instrument, 'a muzzled buzzard' they called it. This caused the inventor to add a device, a metal key, a 'speaker key' he named it, which enabled it to gain a second octave, a strangled muzzled buzzard for those still without an ear for it. Yet, for its growing number of fans, it was a gift straight from heaven. Indeed, from B-flat below middle C, then upward for twenty-two octaves, it was nothing short of a miracle. With the addition of an extra hole, it became unsurpassed in its level of performance."

Who was this amazing inventor, they all wanted to know now? Who was this Benjamin Franklin of the oboe?

"In a moment," N. Emopee. "I mentioned that the oboe began as a candle, which explained why people at first tried to light it. Yet, when, finally, the oboe was made out of wood, it created a whole new set of problems. For instance, the house carpenter at the Pittsburgh Performing Arts Center mistook one for a spindle and installed it into the railing of the grand staircase."

As for who this hippie was who invented the oboe in Pittsburgh, "It is not known," N. Emopee confessed, because there was no such thing.

With this, everyone wanted the entire tour. N. Emopee had done his job.

Rufus took on a laid-off supermarket warehouse manager to, well, help them out, signing him for two weeks for starters. Unbeknownst to N. Emopee, Rufus had had his eye out for a helper for a while now, a minimum-wage worker to keep up with the painting jobs lining up once more, and to increase his profit. N. Emopee liked the change at first, Buster, the new man, the junior man now, the one stuck with all the rolling and the wasps.

N. Emopee's salvation was his full-length film. Never mind that he had started it a dozen times and only barely had it going even now. The problem was, he could not settle on the specifics. Images and feelings were all he had, which resulted in countless wasted writing days, which drove him out of his mind.

Compounding it was his obsession with the mystical, what inspired him the most, how to get at it, how to express it, even though seeking it was futile, by all accounts. Such things were not got at by any means, much less put into words, although the likes of Madame Blavatsky, the Theosophist, had tried. Never mind that his previous writing in this area was, by his own estimation, unproduceable, leaving the likelihood that his film would be the same. Still, he felt he should write what inspired him.

In the meantime, he phoned that executive v.p. whose name and number were on the letter he received the previous week. Were they ready to interview him for that alternative oboing job, corporate oboing, they mentioned?

"We're terribly sorry," the v.p., Mr. Moontooth, said, when, by a miracle, N. Emopee was allowed to speak with him directly. "You see, you are the wrong N. Emopee. Our bad."

How many N. Emopees could there be, N. Emopee had to wonder, much less another N. Emopee looking for alternative oboing? Then, it was a big country, he supposed, more than one Felix Moontooth, too, probably, not that this made him feel any better. More likely, Moontooth just got cold feet, which N. Emopee would, too, knowing what currently he knew about himself.

"A prince in India asked his jeweler to craft a ring for him." This was Ed the painter. "He wanted an inscription on it that would carry him in both good times and bad. When, at last, the jeweler presented the ring to the prince, it contained the words, 'It will pass.'"

N. Emopee liked it. "I like it," he said.

As it happened, Ed was painting a new handrail out front of the house, after the latest group of tourists, fifty bodybuilders from Weirton, visited. Posing for a group picture at the old handrail, they flexed their biceps in unison, and tore the whole thing out.

"If you won't tell us who invented the oboe in Pittsburgh, then at least tell us who wrote music for it?" This was a different group N. Emopee had just given his routine to.

"Okay. Purcell, in the seventeenth century, composed for it."

A look of bewilderment. "We thought you said the oboe was invented in 1968. How could music be written for it in the seventeenth century? It would mean Purcell composed music for an instrument that didn't exist yet."

"Correct. I had not invented it yet. Yes, I am the inventor of the oboe in Pittsburgh in '68."

An image from a dream, a mystical dream, turned out to be the setting, the first detail, of N. Emopee's full-length film. The afterlife it was, a remote land populated only by the protagonist "William," who found himself in a bone-like white stage house, a skull theatre, where he was to play out his mystical issues. This was, N. Emopee had to admit, a long way from that little tale of his about a covert operation led by himself to bring down an invading foreign army.

He got the idea from a program he heard late one night on a public radio station, which, like public television knew all there was to know about everything. At first he could not figure out what it was, inasmuch as it seemed to be a short-wave radio exchange between an interviewer and a scientist. The latter's voice faded in and out as if coming from a great distance. This scientist, it was revealed, was deceased, or so he claimed, the radio program a continuation of his physical world research into electronic communication between the living and the dead.

Whatever the truth of it, it was sufficiently compelling for N. Emopee to send $6.95 to the Parascience Council, who then sent him a copy of this audio tape, including a transcript of it, and an array of literature describing the enormous scientific breakthrough that this research represented. All this was perplexing to N. Emopee because if it was so significant, why wasn't it in all the newspapers and on the evening news.

As he read through the packet of information, though, he noted how other books and pamphlets were also available from this organization, material at no small price, including foundation membership for a truly hefty fee, so that his eventual suspicion that it was a scam, was confirmed. He'd have felt ripped off by it, or felt somehow that it was payback for his b.s. to the tourists at his house, had it not given him the idea for his film, worth far more to him than the $6.95.

The film had to be good enough to be produced, and the sooner the better, because N. Emopee needed the proceeds now to keep away his latest creditor, another of his dad's creditors, the plumbing contractor. Two years prior, after finding fatal cracks in the pool in the basement, Boris drained it. Rem, however, was unable to pay him for what was an emergency service, so the contractor accepted a negotiation. This was the reason why the terra cotta fountain in the herb garden on the west side, back when there was an herb garden on the west side, or, for that matter, even a west side, went off in the plumber's truck.

And then there was the man at his door that same evening, Nestor Hestormantle, the local lawyer whom N. Emopee had hired to save him from the bank. Hestormantle was to argue for Chapter Eleven bankruptcy, to save the house from becoming Mickey Mountain. What neither of them knew, however--Hestormantle was from neighboring Kentucky--was that bankruptcy in West Virginia, Chapter Eleven or any other chapter, didn't existed. West Virginians were too proud ever to admit to bankruptcy, even though most of them were in it. So now the one who was supposed to save him from his creditors was himself a creditor, whom he couldn't afford to pay either. An I.O.U. would have to do.

The heartiness of the pomegranate trees at the mansion was due to their source, the Island of Emopee. Rem revisited the island for his sixtieth birthday and returned with cuttings which here all these years later yielded this amazing grove. Indeed, all the varieties here in the States, the Balegal, the Cloud, the Green Globe, the Phoenicia, the Wonderful, fourteen of them in all, were no match for the Emopee Pomegranate, which in sweetness was unsurpassed. Was it any wonder that visitors to the house happily forked over what was now twelve dollars for a bag of the fruit to take home with them?

And who should be doing this selling but Cleo, feeling more herself these days thanks to Cookie-Aid, that stripped pill for bad cookies. For those needing change, since the actual cost of the pomegranates was $11.95, she had on her money changer, that metal machine with the four tubes, quarters, dimes, nickels, and pennies, left over from 1955 when she drove for the Osgood Bus Line.

Twenty pages into the full-length film and again the whole thing collapsed. He couldn't get it to work. Either it was going to be a film or it was going to be mysticism. It couldn't be both, as he seemed to be attempting to do. Drawn, dejected, demoralized, he headed back to Hick's Used Bookstore for relief in Plato's Cave, where, like the seeker of truth in Plato's story of the cave, he wondered whether he, too, in his quest to become a successful anything in the biz, wasn't mistaking shadows for reality.

The beady electric eye at Hick's followed him all the way down High Street, was lying in wait for him, knowing as it did that N. Emopee was distressed, so that the moment he entered the store it beeped loudly, louder than usual, sending him to the ceiling almost, prompting Bert to bark his head off just for good measure. Luckily, Mr. Hick was at the front counter to restore order, a short leash for a long walk, but not before a severe scolding of Bert in front of everyone, which made N. Emopee feel even worse.

Having lost his taste for books on mysticism, suddenly, N. Emopee decided to stop at the drama section over from the front counter, because drama, in light of that drama class he took that time, to say nothing of his term paper on Ghelderode, sentimental executioners and all that, he knew about, was competent in, had confidence regarding.

It so happened that a play by Strindberg, *The Road to Damascus*, was the first book he came to, his Coke-bottle glasses getting a nudge and his arthritic left ring finger a tuck. Which was when he noticed out of the corner of his eye, Raymond, Mr. Hick's teenage grandson, gaunt and gangly as always, at the front counter. Raymond, though, was unaccustomed to seeing this familiar patron in the drama aisle, prompting him to give N. Emopee a strange stare as only Raymond could give.

What this really was was Raymond's curiosity. Was this man looking at Strindberg over there a theatrical producer, possibly, or a film and television actor-director-producer, a biz SOMEBODY? Reluctant to push himself on N. Emopee, not without his mother anyway, Raymond accepted that all he could do was stand there, anxiously teeter there, at the counter, red-faced, pimply-mouthed, where he was left to resume applying brodarts, plastic protective sheets, to the pile of hardcover dust jackets in front of him.

But just then N. Emopee discovered next to the Strindberg play an old edition of Maeterlinck's play *The Bluebird*. Now, N. Emopee was never enthusiastic about this fairy tale, preferring the playwright's earlier mood plays, static or inner drama as they were called, stories which, as the back cover described, "depicted human spiritual loneliness and sense of helplessness in the face of the occult forces of destiny."

Thumbing through *The Bluebird*, he was about to put it back when what should fall out it but two loose newspaper clippings, both dated 1909. Were they really in this book for 91 years? One was from *The San Francisco Examiner* and the other from the *New York Times*, both of them regarding the American debut of what then was the latest Maeterlinck play.

N. Emopee, thrilled, hauled the book to Raymond, who was all excited now, too, a chance to chat with this actor-director-producer.

"I don't want to buy this book, Raymond, a little short of cash just now, but I wondered if I could have these two newspaper clippings that dropped out of it."

As though they were dead animals, Raymond grimaced, then shrugged matter-of-factly. "People find things in books here all the time," he confessed. "Mr. Schaumer, who comes in every Monday afternoon, found a twenty-dollar bill in the pages of a 1951 *Roget's Thesaurus*. Mr. Hick says finder's keepers."

Even though he didn't know what he was going to do with them exactly, N. Emopee refolded the articles gently, then slid them into his left-hand shirt pocket. All he knew was, there was something about them, a "vibration." They inspired him.

"Thanks, Raymond. Did you know that Maeterlinck, whom these clippings are about, hated to travel by boat? This, the clippings said, was why his attending the New York premier of his newest play was out of the question."

Raymond squinted. The fact was, Raymond had never heard of Maeterlinck so didn't care whether the guy showed up for the first performance of his play in New York, or anywhere else for that matter, or not. Finally, "Here's an envelope for them if you'd like." Raymond held out a little clear plastic packet.

On N. Emopee's good side, now, Raymond decided the time was ripe for seizing the moment, to satisfy his curiosity, to rid himself of the nagging question, his best shot coming out approximately, "Will those clippings be for your new show?"

"My new show?"

"I thought maybe you were a producer or something, theatre maybe, looking for ideas, planning your next show."

"There could be a show in them, I suppose, 'Maurice Maeterlinck Revisited,' but it won't be by me."

Raymond, mouth down, but then up again, "A film maybe?"

"Not by me."

"You're not a movie producer?"

Recalling Popcorn Pictures, where had he signed up with Crump that time he might well be by now, N. Emopee smiled, ironically. "No."

"You're a professor then," Raymond, persistently.

"What is this, 'Twenty Questions'?"

Raymond, another blush, "It's just that I'm in our school play, you see, and I thought you might be somebody important."

N. Emopee, hands up, "No. Nobody important."

Back to his brodarts, as if N. Emopee had left the room, Raymond yawned.

"I could be a teacher, though," N. Emopee, after another moment. "I have a college degree."

Raymond, as if to say, "Well, why aren't you then?"

"Except it's not my temperament. Students would be worse off by their exposure to me."

Raymond had never heard of such a thing and put his skinny hands on his skinny hips.

"But now then," N. Emopee, a minute longer, "what if I was somebody important, as you put it? What would you want from me?"

"What would I want?" Raymond with a blink.

"I mean, do you want to be a movie star?"

A giggle. Raymond had read all the "teen zines," how kids just like him had been discovered, so to say, by producers and directors in just such unexpected places as this.

"It's not what people think it is, you know," N. Emopee, honestly. "From what I've seen, it's more trouble than it's worth."

"I've never heard that," Raymond, quickly.

"Eight years ago I worked in film and television in Pittsburgh, as a stagehand, with the advantage of seeing it all behind the scenes. I was from me to you to Dan Ackroyd, Gilda Radner, Harry Belafonte, Artie Johnson, William Shatner, Dom Delouise, Christopher Plummer, Kaye Ballard, Donald Sutherland, to name just a few, and from what I saw, being a star is a drag most of the time."

Raymond was not taking N. Emopee's word for it. "Really?"

"So who got you to go out for your school play? Jules?"

Raymond, "It's required.

"Oh. Well, I'm just glad it wasn't required when I was your age."

"Why's that?"

"I'm shy. Capital S-H-Y."

"I don't mind it."

A pivot for the door and N. Emopee was on his way, but not before, "I'm a screenwriter you may as well know, to answer your question."

Raymond, eyes wide suddenly, was impressed.

"That's right. A screenwriter."

But why did N. Emopee reveal this to Raymond when he didn't know yet whether he was a screenwriter or not? Well, the answer was plain enough. Dawning on him while he was engaged there with Raymond, the idea of Maeterlinck. He would make his full-length film an inner drama, an inner film, depicting human spiritual loneliness and sense of helplessness in the face of the occult forces of destiny.

His head cocked severely to the left, N. Emopee tugged open the glass emergency-room door at the nearby Morganhill Intercommunity Hospital, where it was 2:30 in the morning. Only two other people were inside, in the waiting room, a young expectant mother, and, by the look of him, judging by his doting on her, her husband. Behind a small window with a small hole in the center of it, a box office window at a movie theater it looked like, and into which N. Emopee was to speak, hovered a receptionist with very fat arms. His face contorted N. Emopee got scarcely a look from this woman, who went straight to it. "Do you have insurance?"

Dazed and not knowing what he was saying, N. Emopee answered that, yes, he did, whereupon he gave the name of his car insurance company, the only insurance company of his that he could think of just then. Actually, he could no longer afford health insurance, hadn't had health insurance since leaving Stiff Arm, but he didn't recall this just then. That his auto insurance company also happened to offer health coverage proved a lucky break because the receptionist didn't question him on it.

When at last, mercifully, her pen reached the bottom of the form she was filling out, Mrs. Wirk, Opal Wirk her name tag read, nodded to him to have a seat. "A doctor will see you presently," she said.

N. Emopee, if he could have, would have nodded to her in return, but he departed instead for an orange plastic chair in the far corner. Dropping onto it, he abruptly dropped back up, any settling of his body, at his shoulders in particular, an electric shock the way it felt to him. It was the same for him in his apartment an hour earlier when he tried to go to bed despite this, thinking it would go away on its own, but it only made it worse. His catapulting back to his feet caught the attention of the expectant mother, who now had the hiccups.

Which gave N. Emopee the idea that a cool drink of water might take his mind off his suffering, so down the hall to the water fountain he dragged himself, a slow bus ride across town it might as well have been. The fountain, however, when at last he got to it, proved to be one of the recessed kind, set into the wall, to where his head, far over to the left in spasm, would not fit in. As a result, all he could do was stand there, stand, then pace painfully, stop, stand, and pace some more.

Of all the things for him to do, though, he chastised himself once again. How could he think that doing what he did wouldn't injure him in some predictable way? "Simply," in defense of himself, his lips moving silently, "it was something I'd never done before, something I did naively, innocently, without thinking about it, without suspecting what it would lead to."

His bloodshot eyes shifted to the couple down the way, on their own orange plastic chairs, the woman as round as a vat, the man just as pregnant, one beer too many by the look of him. Still in her glass box, meantime, Mrs. Wirk was positioned now in such a way that her nose was opposite the small hole in her window, a target at a carnival game to see it. N. Emopee would have laughed, wanted to laugh, but the price was too high to pay.

With the passing of a seeming eternity, there appeared, finally, a nurse. From the swinging double doors of the treatment room she called out into blank space, "Mr. N. Emopee?"

N. Emopee dove ahead as best he could.

A rectangular curtained enclosure was their destination, but not before the nurse, who had been observing him askance the entire time, made out with the obvious question, "What happened to you?"

N. Emopee searched for words through his misery, but not so much as a shrug from him, certainly not a shrug.

"Here," the nurse, "put on this hospital gown. I'll get the doctor."

Alone in the enclosure with the neatly folded pale blue gown, N. Emopee just stood there, half stood and half leaned against the gurney, parked as it was on his right side, beside him. Put that on? She couldn't be serious.

Just then the curtains parted suddenly and, Johnny Carson fashion, in strode the doctor, his right hand outstretched in greeting, which N. Emopee, in a reflex, reached for, only to pay the heavy price. "Owwww," he cried out.

Simultaneous apologies, "Sorry," "Pardon me," "Excuse me," "Forgive me."

"What's the trouble here, son?" the doctor, his stethoscope to N. Emopee's chest now, not where the problem was, whereupon he tried a firm feel around the neck, the real issue, a neck that shuddered with every diagnostic grip. "How did this happen?"

"Writing screenplays can be hazardous to your health," N. Emopee, struggling at levity. "I leaned too hard on my left elbow while my head was at this angle--for six hours."

"Screenwriter neck, yes. I see it all the time here in Hollywoods. I'll have the nurse give you a painkiller, a muscle relaxant and a painkiller. You can put on that gown in the meantime."

N. Emopee peered at the garment again, in dismay.

When the nurse came back into the room, a rubber tourniquet and syringe in tow, what she found was an N. Emopee in the pale blue gown sure enough, only it was on backwards, like an overcoat.

"You've never been to a hospital before have you, Mr. Emopee?" She handed him another gown from a nearby shelf. "Try it again."

N. Emopee got it right the second time, no more peak-a-booing privates, even if the second looked like the other half of the first, which he still had on. He looked in a clam shell.

When the nurse returned, she tied the tourniquet around the soft side of his left forearm, which then, to ready it for the needle, got a wipe with an alcohol puff. But as the room was 65 degrees, chilly for just a hospital gown, for two hospital gowns even, no vein was willing to show itself. "No vein," the nurse said. N. Emopee assured her that he had one.

"Here, I'll try it this way." The nurse paused a minute then snuck up on a vein from behind. Bingo, she nailed it.

When the doctor turned up again, he found his patient still half standing, half leaning on the gurney, where he appeared to be contemplating a hookah-like affair at the wall in the corner, a stomach pump, which, in light of all the medication just administered to him, looked awfully appealing.

"So, how did it go?" the doctor, peering at his eyes. He then placed his hands again on N. Emopee's neck.

Righting N. Emopee's head was like straightening the Leaning Tower of Pisa, it turned out--"Owwww"--so that, "I'll have the nurse give you another round," a bullet to his head the way it sounded. Accordingly, in came the nurse and ten minutes later, N. Emopee was jello. So loose was he, in fact, that the neck brace, the thick padded kind as used for whiplash, that the doctor came back with, curled on him like a snake around a pole. "You'll have relief soon enough, Mr. Emopee," the doctor, reassuringly, with a smile. But not before, "I hear you can make a lot of money at screenwriting."

The question was now, though, how was N. Emopee going to get home? "I can't recommend that you drive in your current state," the doctor, staring again at his eyes. "On the other hand, once you walk out this door, there's nothing I can do."

N. Emopee, in the end, did indeed drive himself home, but by way of Fairfield.

Chapter Nine
Scott Merriweather Literary Agency

*D*espite the collar and the prescription painkillers, N. Emopee's neck ached for all of the following week. Lost were his painting days, which, throwing off his work schedule, vexed Rufus beyond words. And in that he needed the painting money to pay off his latest creditor, the cleaning lady, even though she hadn't worked for him in a year, infuriated N. Emopee as well.

As for his writing days, these were a wash, too, the mind-dulling prescription the doctor gave him blanking his usually bountiful imagination so that not one word found one page in his screenplay. Never mind that the meaning of his full-length film, remembering that he insisted that it be about something, not just nothing, he no longer understood. Even the idea of making it Maeterlinckian seemed silly to him now, not worth his effort. Consequently he made no progress on it for another two weeks. In short, the prospect of his becoming a successful screenwriter, making lots of money, either in film or television, was utterly out the window. And with it, all prospects of his converting the house into a refuge for remnants of foreign wars, his sworn obligation to Rem, came to a screeching halt.

Which was when Rufus gave him the ultimatum that if he didn't make up the painting days he'd lost, he'd have to fire him. But when N. Emopee was finally able to complete the work, painting for two weeks straight, including weekends, he felt like only a painter again, which plunged him into even deeper despair.

This was when the selling of One Pound Down Street occurred to him once more, except that Thor Snover, the bank manager, reminded him that the bank had a lien on the place, to cover not only his, N. Emopee's, debt to them, but his dad's as well. "It's a miracle we even let you sleep here any longer," admitted Snover.

Then, out of nowhere, there was this in his journal:

When I awoke this morning I found myself identity-less, without ego. As I talked I didn't know who it was doing the talking. My speech was like an alien language, the creation of which seemed little more than the beating together of two sticks. I no longer

related to the play or the players. My heart pounded,
my limbs shook, and my throat turned as dry as stone.
I lost it.

In some circles, this was a mystical experience, in others insanity.

N. Emopee found himself reminiscing about his exile in Erie eight years earlier, and about the final three days of it in particular, his time first with Rita, then with Amy, and finally with Estella, girl friends all, even though he didn't like girls. Was he feeling lonely now with all his troubles? It had to do with his financial problems, yes, but even more so with his becoming a writer, the risk of it, and how isolated it made him feel. While he dreamed of being an artist one day even up in Erie, where he penned the odd story now and then, his better judgment told him to leave writing alone. It told him that staying "grounded," remaining firmly in touch with reality, was healthier for him than a life in his imagination. And didn't Rita, Amy, and Estella, despite his poor relations with them, help him to maintain this grounding; wasn't it the sanest time of his life?

How then should he feel about this period he was currently in, having both feet on the ground hardly how he would characterize it. Should he feel proud of risking everything for what he'd come to believed was the right thing for him to do, screenwriting, or would he see himself a fool, see that he had overestimated his talent and underestimated his need to be like everybody else? Eunice wanted him to be safe and predictable, like Rem was, with a regular job and income, something other than oboing, much less screenwriting, and she may well have been right.

Well, naturally, it all depended on whether or not over time he was successful at his writing, although as an artist this shouldn't matter really, his happiness in just doing the work the reward. "Ah, that it were as simple as this," to himself now, for it rather seemed he had passed the point of no return.

When he left his full-length film he had the protagonist William discovering in the stage house of the afterlife, a room containing costumes, which William saw not as costumes but as worldly ego-identities, the illusion of which was William's central issue. It was the break-through N. Emopee was looking for.

The completion of his film a week later was a triumph for him beyond description, a work not a mishmash, as he worried it might be, but a continuous story involving one protagonist with a specific issue. Only in his wildest dreams did he believe he would actually pull it off, so that in his own eyes, at least, he was now a successful screenwriter.

The downside was that it was a crumb to a starving man. It left him craving more, the last thing a person with his marginal talent needed.

The day after he finished his film, a brochure arrived in his mailbox, or in his mason jar, what passed for his mailbox these days, from the Scott Merriweather Literary Agency. It was a mystery where they got his name, and how it happened to appear at precisely this moment. That this was the doing of that stream he felt himself drifting in, his grip securely on that mystical log, was a temptation he found hard to resist.

It was a signal to him, maybe, that he should submit his film, *The William Film*, to this agency. It would be for the purpose of getting it produced, making him not only a legitimate screenwriter but a celebrity as well, if not a star. That it was his ticket to saving his house was the big promise, though, the thought of which made his head spin.

Eunice, a Christian Scientist, came down on the side of divine guidance, prompting her, after he made the case to her in the strongest terms, to lend him $500 of her savings, half of which would go to his new typist Marge, the other half to the agency, for their evaluation of the screenplay. This would be followed later by the producing of it, if he was lucky, and, if he was truly blessed, a world premiere of it, in New York, possibly, like Maeterlinck.

Yet there was a problem, a major problem, as he read the brochure again, especially the last paragraph. They handled only novels, not screenplays, it said. In fact, as he looked further into it, researched it at the library the next day, he found that not one of the literary agencies out there represented film scripts either. Just novels. Or books, rather. Fiction and nonfiction. This was the last thing he needed.

He should take a cue from the memoir he just read, *I REFUSE, Memories of a Vietnam War Objector.* That book the author shopped around for two years before ultimately it was published. The difference was that he, N. Emopee, didn't have the luxury of a year. He needed help right away, needed someone to expedite the process for him. Then again, if agents were not accepting screenplays, what was he to do? What he was to do was become an agent himself, in which case he could return Eunice's money to her, which he would very much like to do. But how do you become an agent?

At the Palace of Pump, where he met Mr. Snavely that time, Snavely of the public television station, N. Emopee circled the jogging track with a retired savings and loan manager he had known for two years now, a man originally from Pittsburgh.

"So how's the oboing going?" Mr. Gilley, Rudder Gilley, asked him.

"Oboing going? I'm no longer oboing, as I'm sure I told you already."

Gilley had hard black eyes and white hair, so that he looked like a snowman with coal for eyes. He was well aware of N. Emopee's current struggles, indeed wasn't he one of those at the gym who considered him a fool for not becoming a community college teacher like his dad, then a dunce for trying to get into "alternative oboing" in film and television, and now an idiot for attempting to be a screenwriter. That he enjoyed N. Emopee struggling all this time was

because it made his own success in the savings and loan business appear even more so, which in a gym full of egomaniacs was highly desirable.

"The last time I saw you, I explained to you that I was now writing screenplays. Well, I'm not doing that anymore now either."

"Oh, good. Or rather sorry to hear it."

They were strolling twice around the track to cool down, the retiree just having finished an exercise bike, N. Emopee the jump rope he'd bought the year before and had just now learned how to use.

"I've written a novel, you see." N. Emopee was converting his screenplay into a novel. Whatever it took.

The man, in surprise, smiled once. "You don't say. Goodness me."

"I'm getting it typed professionally in Fairfield. I want it to look professional."

"I thought you had a typist here in Morganhill."

"Emily's Typical Typing no longer exists. Emily is with the police department now."

"Really? Officer Emily?"

"Ever since Chief Federer had her type his barbeque cookbook, *Cop Chops*, he's been trying to get her to be their receptionist. A regular paycheck now appealed to her, she told me, a house full of pets she had to feed, and she was facing a hike in her rent.   This was to say nothing of the big car payment she had for the new Chevy she just bought. But, finally, she was just tired of the business, she said to me. She wanted a change."

"You're not a good typist yourself? You could save yourself a lot of money by doing it yourself," to be expected from a savings and loan man.

"No, I don't type. My left ring finger is arthritic, as you can see, to where I'm not only missing a note on my oboe, but the letter 's' on the typewriter as well. And then, as luck would have it, my right ring finger has arched out of alignment, too, see?" his right hand up, "so that now I am missing the letter 'l' also, and do you have any idea how many 's's and 'l's there are in a novel?"

"A lot," Gilley.

"Oh, I could peck away with my right pointer finger, like my dad and Beckett used to do. I mean it's not as if I don't know where the letters are. It's just that typing a full novel this way would take me six months, and I don't have that kind of time."

"Have you tried an Arth-Rite pill?"

"By the way, Emily said that it was my job search in the biz, looking for alternative oboing, that contributed to her change, the same with my friend Jon Doh at the American Film Institute. He now has his own freelance researching business, 'Let Doh Do It,' customers lined up down the street. You can imagine how that makes me feel."

"Proud?"

"Lousy."

"Oh, lousy."

"Because they're doing better than I am. But only for the moment. My odds have just improved."

"You said your new typist lives in Fairfield?"

"That's right."

"In the desert?"

"What's wrong with the desert?"

"But why all the way down there?"

"It's not that far. Thirty-five minutes."

"Thirty-five minutes is thirty-five minutes," Gilley profoundly.

"The truth is," N. Emopee, frankly, "I wanted to get someone with a background in novels, a person who knows how to type dialogue. My novel has a lot of dialogue, and Marge has this. She typed *Lawrence of Fairfield*, you know, which is all dialogue."

"You don't say."

They halted long enough for the retiree to rub his knees. He had had surgery for bow-leggedness, legs bowed outward, the year before, but here these twelve months later, they were bowed again, only in the opposite direction. "But there must be tons of novels-with-dialogue typists up this way, closer to Morganhill," Gilley, a minute later.

"There aren't."

"How did you know to go with this Marge?"

N. Emopee flinched, cringed and then flinched, for in point of fact, he chose Marge psychically, the feel of her over the phone," not easy to explain, and certainly not to Gilley. "Let's just say I found her," and he left it at that. "And when the novel is ready, I'm sending it to a literary agency."

"How interesting. How did you find <u>them</u>?"

This was even worse. "I found them, let's just say, or rather they found me."

Stepping to the steps leading down to the showers, where the retiree was headed, they stopped. "Well, at least with an agency they tell you right away whether you're any good, so you can get on with your life before wasting any more of it."

Insensitive remarks like this from Gilley he had grown used to, to the extent that he expected them, as he did from Rufus. If he didn't get them, he felt shortchanged.

"It is not what others do and do not do that is my concern." Ed the painter was quoting the Buddhist *Dhammapada*. "It is what *I* do and do not do. *This* is my concern."

"Mine too, Ed."

When N. Emopee returned to painting with Rufus the following Monday, it was to the news that his uncle was disbanding the crew. N. Emopee and the new man, Buster, would be out on the street at the end of the week. Why was Rufus doing this? The business was making lots of money, as evidenced by Rufus' new Honda, red with a stick shift. They were settled into a routine and were content together. The only conclusion that N. Emopee could come up with was that it was something to do with <u>him</u>. He wasn't sure what it could be, something to do with his completing one of his writing projects, maybe, which his uncle, like Gilley, assumed would never come about, and now that it had, was a threat to him.

But if he, N. Emopee, was to blame, why fire Buster? Then, wasn't it typical of Rufus's shotgun approach to solving problems, a heavy-handedness that he picked up from his father, Otto. Otto was of the "if-it-doesn't-move-paint-it" school of house painting, a man for whom life was an obstacle, a thing not to be maneuvered through with skill, but to be run over like a bulldozer.

In his damage control mode, N. Emopee struggled with how to handle this impending job loss, finishing with what could only be a shotgun solution of his own. "For the past three weeks," he wrote in his journal that same night, "I have felt energies coming to a head in me, as if the completion of a cycle, the final conclusion of rising, zenith, and ebb, to where I have decided to go for broke. Instead of submitting to the agency only *The William Novel*, as I now call it, I will also send them my story from Erie, that covert operation one, and then, for good measure, my best poetry. If I can get these represented and sold, the loss of my painting job will be irrelevant."

To this end he borrowed an additional $150 from Eunice, saying this time, "It's God's plan for me," even though it was the greatest risk he had taken in his life. As for Eunice and why she would let herself be coerced again this way, let her son play on her faith this way, the answer was the novel itself. She had read it by now, as much of it that was available, and honestly liked it. "The only thing missing is a Eunice character," she laughed to him. "Then, it's your novel not mine. And if the rest of your writing is as good as this, I won't stand in your way."

His package of writing in the mail to Scott Merriweather, N. Emopee set his mind to his next project. In his next novel, *The Knower*, he would explore theosophy, "a subject I was introduced to three months ago," he wrote in his journal, "while researching the afterlife for *The William Novel*."

Theosophy, theosophical speculation, centered on mystical experience, to include esoteric doctrine, the deciphering of hidden meaning concealed in sacred texts, and occult phenomena. Monism, according to Madame Blavatsky, the founder of the theosophical movement, was its orientation, the view that reality was constituted of one principle: mind or spirit. Generally it was in line with Asian thought such as Vedanta and Buddhism, which sealed it for N. Emopee.

In his journal, he added, "Theosophy is the realm of the unspoken-unspeakable, which paradoxically for me, a writer, is not communicable either, that is to say, is not expressible in words so much as revealed in the spaces between words. My new novel will have a lot of spaces in it."

Further inspiring this new book was a notebook of his, less a notebook than a series of drawings rendered by him when he was seventeen years old. Midway through this collection was a figure which, as he described it then, was an attempt to visually represent his essence, as he felt it to be at the time. It was an arrangement of lines which touched at an axis, and which were two-dimensional as drawn, but three-dimensional in appearance, a metaphor. Indeed, coming upon it now at thirty-four years old, he saw immediately that it was a yantra, a mystical representation of the Atman, the cosmic true self, as reflective of the godhead Brahman.

Also among the drawings was a circle bisected by a sigmoid line, his conception of the dynamic of the universe, even though he had not yet been exposed to the Asian idea, and image, of the Yin and Yang.

There was a saying that when a person was ready for a guru, one would turn up, and so it was that while painting the side of a house in east Morganhill, N. Emopee, the ear buds of his radio firmly in his ears, picked up the voice of one Alan Watts on a public radio station. Rufus, as it happened, had not yet disbanded the crew. Now Watts was not a guru, never claiming to be one, which was to say that he was not a spiritual teacher associated with a specific religion. Yet in every other way, he _was_ one, and a philosopher, scholar, and author. Along with D. T. Suzuki, he introduced Zen to the West. N. Emopee now had his guru.

"So let's hear it," Rufus with a grin the following afternoon while he, Buster, and N. Emopee were painting a kitchen too small for the three of them, except that it was all they had to do that day.

"Pardon me?" N. Emopee popped the ear buds from his ears.

"I say, how about letting us hear your program?"

Now, Rufus becoming interested in eastern philosophy was as likely as a turtle becoming interested in the Gettysburg Address. Rather it was a "radio game" where if Rufus listened to N. Emopee's program, then N. Emopee was obliged to listen to Rufus', which was a radio psychologist named Dr. Laurie Linslinger, or Laurie Shitslinger as N. Emopee called her to himself, who drove N. Emopee nuts.

"You wouldn't like Watts," N. Emopee, killing this at the start, hopefully.

Buster, for his part, was a Golden Oldies man, so he didn't want to hear either program.

"No, I'm curious what it is," Rufus, his hairy hand over his hairless head.

To keep his uncle from making a scene, as he did when he was denied a game he particularly wanted to play, N. Emopee yielded in the end. And so they all listened to Watts speak about the false perception of the continuity of life, produced by memory. It was like rotating a burning branch in the air, creating the illusion of a continuous circle when, in fact, it was a ring of moments.

Well, after the first minute of this it was evident that Rufus had not a clue what this was about, while Buster, hearing no Golden Oldies, just squirmed. But as the program went on,

Buster became increasingly agitated, huffing and grumbling and knocking things around, prompting N. Emopee to reach now for the on-off switch.

By now, though, it was clear that Rufus' thoughts really were on Dr. Laurie, whose program was coming up next, on his radio.

"If this is, that comes to be; from the arising of this, that arises; if this is not, that does not come to be; from the stopping of this, that stops," the Buddhist teaching went. N. Emopee thereafter left his radio at home.

To help him make ends meet, and in light of his kitchen that was no more, emptied by the appliance man to pay him off, he became a vegan. No longer eating meat, eggs, or dairy, it had the added benefit of making him feel like a monk. Rice and potatoes were the centerpiece of his new regimen, the latter easy enough to bake in his old microwave oven--he still had that--although when he tried it with the rice he ended up with rice crispies.

His subsequent weight loss did not go unnoticed by Cleo. "You are a mere shadow of your former self, Nathan, which considering you were a shadow to begin with, all in all, well, I'm worried about you. "

"I'm fine, Cleo. Fine." If anything, N. Emopee was worried about her, not because of any diet she was on, but because he rarely saw her anymore. Was she going the way of all his other friends, not the least of whom were Jon

Doh the researcher, and Emily of Typical Typing? Was she striking out on her own?

In Cleo's case he could understand it. She was busy. The conducting of tours at the house, what was left of it, was Cleo's fulltime job now, not because he had asked it of her, not anymore, but because she wanted to do it. It inspired her. "You're the writer, I'm the guide," she joked to him all the time. She was like a kid who took an acting class only to discover that she had talent. "I've created a monster," admitted N. Emopee. Why he had this effect on people was beyond him, forgetting that he had the same effect on himself, the biggest monster of them all? He could only hope that Cleo fared better at it than him.

"Nathan," Cleo to the point now, the reason she tracked him down just then, "during this morning's tour I opened the drawer to your father's desk, what is left of it, and I found these blue prints. Do you have any idea what they are of? I'd like to show them off to tomorrow's group."

"Is that Old Spice aftershave you are wearing, Cleo?"

"I've never seen blue prints around here before," said Cleo.

"Or Brut. Yes, that's it. Why are you wearing Brut?"

"Here, look."

Cleo rolled open the roll of blue paper carefully, since it appeared it had been rolled up for 30 years.

"Likely it has something to do with Rem's patent for 'suck-tite,' the rubber rings for canning jars he invented, before his running shoes caught on. Let me see them."

"'Suck-tite?'"

"His rubber seals for canning jars. I told you about them."

"A product should never have the word 'suck' in it."

"Never mind, Cleo."

On rolling the prints out they found not a bunch of circles as would be expected, but floor plans, three of them. And at the bottom of each, the words "refuge for foreign war remnants," in Rem's own longhand.

"Oh," N. Emopee, his coke-bottle glasses getting a shove.

"Oh?"

"Oh, oh." Because the discovery was the first glimpse of how precisely Rem envisioned the refuge. This was the good news. The bad part, of course, was that it had yet to be realized, and would never be realized the way things were going. Cleo scratched her head with a crow bone, an oboe crow bone, she had stuck in her hair.

As N. Emopee savored the plans, which included an indoor basketball court, and a cafeteria in place of the existing kitchen, he was reminded that Rem had done nothing either to further the cause. His problem was that he had gotten himself into so much debt. Even when he had money he was short of it.

An eight-page evaluation of the package of writing N. Emopee sent to Scott Merriweather arrived one week later. In the assessment Mr. Merriweather deemed *The William Novel* "impenetrable." As for his early story, that covert operation tale from Erie, it was "nothing that hasn't been written a hundred times before only more effectively." As for his poems, these were "the least successful of the lot."

He did allow, however, that N. Emopee had "a rich imagination," and "skill with words," and that "your writing has a high degree of polish," but at the end of the day "another line of work might be better for you."

Mr. Merriweather's wish to not bite the hand that fed him was the conspicuous reason for the "rich imagination," "skill with words," and "polish" part of it, evidenced by his subsequent invitation to him to send more writing, with the hefty evaluation fee, naturally. To Mr. Merriweather's credit, he did describe what constituted saleable material in current markets, stories written in classical five-part structure, point of attack, rising action, crisis, climax, and resolution. N. Emopee was familiar already with this from Saul Script and Sherm Bird screenwriting courses. Merriweather added that from what he could see, he, N. Emopee, was not out to write a conventional novel with *The William Novel*, a nice way for him to put it, when in fact he, N. Emopee, didn't know <u>what</u> he was out to write except that he wanted to go from his inner being, the same approach he intended for *The Knower*.

That night N. Emopee dreamed that Rem was chasing him barber pole fashion down the street with an ax.

Chapter Ten
On Again/Off Again Painting Company

"I talked with Rufus last night," N. Emopee to Eunice, "and told him that the Merriweather Agency would not be representing my writing after all. Knowing nothing about artists and the dues they have to pay, he believes that I have failed once and for all, and because I'm no longer a threat to him in whatever way, at least that's how I read it, he's letting me work again."

"Is he letting Buster work too?"

"Yes, he is."

"He's certainly got you by the nape of the neck, doesn't he?" a sadness in Eunice's voice, didn't he heard it the moment she opened her mouth, all to do with his writing-supported-by-painting regime, when there were a multitude of other things he could be doing instead. A gloom was in N. Emopee's voice, too, the result of his having to continue this charade, of having to pretend self-confidence when he knew he was already defeated. Even his "I'll pay you back the money, don't worry," rang hollow.

But Mr. Merriweather stated one other thing in his evaluation, not to be overlooked. "You can write quirky stories if you want, Mr. Emopee, the beauty and significance of which only you, and a few others, possibly, are able to fully appreciate, but if you want to be successful in this business, want to make money at it, you must be more conventional."

Yet, quirky was satisfying to N. Emopee, to his inner being, to the degree that he wondered now whether he shouldn't be a martyr for it. Writing was not the point after all, not in the end. He was not writing just to write, was not writing for the love of it, but to get at, to feel closer to, the mystical. Wasn't this what his life was all about finally? Then he didn't want to paint houses for Rufus forever either, forever after. And without money coming in, and a lot of it real soon, Rem's refuge home, to say nothing of his own, was out the window.

The Knower he decided would describe two different realities occurring simultaneously, with events in the one affecting those in the other, even though, by any stretch of the imagination, even his, it was not a conventional story either. Then, after considering it further, after sleeping on it yet another night, he settled on a compromise. He would set it in one reality only, with just a hint of the other, for as long as he could swing it.

But alas, as he stated in his journal two days later:

This morning I have attempted to write conventionally, but I cannot get past the first page. Why is this so? It's because to write just to write, just to be another entertainer, so to say, is not the reason I'm doing it. With the very first word I could see the whole thing, including myself at the end saying, 'Why did I bother?' My view of the real world is no different, to be honest. From the moment I was born I saw the entire thing, with myself in my last breath saying, 'Why did I bother?'

And with this, *The Knower* was dead in the water, as was, once and for all, N. Emopee's writing career.

Rufus announced two days later that he was terminating the crew all over again, this time on July 1st, and, as before, he gave no reason for it despite insisting that there was one. More than likely it was because his work had dried up, as it did from time to time throughout the year. In light of the deteriorating relations between the three of them, between Buster and N. Emopee in particular, issues about which of them was to do what task, with no direction from Rufus, N. Emopee felt the breakup was for the best.

Still, what would he do when the painting stopped, he worried, Rufus the only commercial painter in Morganhill worth his salt, worth his thinner, and with a customer base to prove it. Who else would he paint for? In his damage control mode once more, his solution was to return to his multi-page resume, to his "ego sheets," as he called them, where he listed his past successes, including his earning his B.O. degree, his Bachelor of Oboing degree. Wait! A flash of insight. The idea occurred to him of a <u>non</u>-teaching job. He could be a facilities manager for oboe concerts, for example. It didn't have to be in college. Surely somewhere in Morganhill, if not in all of West Virginia, there would be something for him.

Then, wasn't West Virginia too narrow of a focus for him? Thus, he subscribed to a twice-monthly employment bulletin called *OBOESEARCH*, which Professor Bag had told him about, and which listed non-teaching jobs in oboing <u>throughout the country</u>. *The Manacle of Higher Education*, which had similar broad listings, he'd subscribe to as well.

And, last but not least, he made an appointment with the chairman of the Oboing Arts department at Westhill Community College across the river, not far from his house, a mere bridge away, twenty minutes door to door. He could see whether there wasn't something for him there, some capacity for him, non-teaching, but then teaching too, a measure of his desperation.

Teaching? The issue of his having no interest in it, temperament, or talent aside, he had no experience at it.

Why let it cross his mind when he knew no one would give him a serious look anyway? Then again, Rem had never done any teaching either, according to Eunice, and he was hired, becoming a full professor by the end of it.

All this felt good to him. He was taking charge, getting back in control of his life, finding solutions to his problems.

But then, out of the blue, Rufus announced his willingness to keep the crew past July 1st, painting work coming in again, money for one and all, "Please come back." It was crazy-making if ever there was. But if N. Emopee did not phone Rufus back on it this time, he was not alone. Buster didn't either. His having a wife and two kids to feed meant he needed a steady, reliable job. As a result he decided to become a painting contractor himself, up in Starville, north of town, where he lived.

For N. Emopee, meantime, it was a case of nothing remotely matching his qualifications in either *OBOESEARCH* or *The Manacle of Higher Education*, albeit it <u>was</u> summertime when jobs were scarce. As for Westhill Community College, they wrote him to say that they would get back to him in August, which was to say, having gotten back to him now, they would get back to him some more later on. Thank goodness he had his income from the tours.

Cleo's coming upon blue prints of the refuge-to-be, Rem's conception of it, brought a tear to N. Emopee's eye. The prints were in Rem's desk, what was left of it, in the north wing. "Odd the affection you have for a father you never knew all that well, not really. I knew him well enough, I guess, but not entirely. But then who knows anyone, themselves included, entirely?

Still, there were memories. Every summer when the staff went on vacation to the south wing, he and April visited Rem in the north wing. It was the only time they ever saw him at that point, since he retired.

Rem was by himself then, by choice. The cleaning lady kept his wing tidy, vacuuming, dusting, while the rest of it, cooking and washing, he handled on his own. Even when N. Emopee and April were with him he prepared all the meals, including theirs, and kept everyone's clothes clean. He even ironed the sheets. N. Emopee and April didn't know you could iron sheets, and had never slept on an ironed sheet before.

Yet, for N. Emopee it was the sounds, the smells of Rem's north wing that lingered in his mind. The tick-tock of the old clock, built by Rem, in the corner, was less a tick-tock than a thump-thump, hard to distinguish from that other thump, the one made by Rem's blind terrier Abigail. She was forever bumping into the furniture.

The other sound in Rem's place was the ever-present chatter of the TV, which back then was Dave Garroway of *The Today Show*, and then Arthur Godfrey on *The Arthur Godrey Show*, and finally *The Howdy Doody Show* with Buffalo Bob and Clarabell.

Then there was the smell of Rem's roses outside his window. Next to the pomegranate grove, they were his proudest accomplishment. They were abundant on his native Emopee Island, but cultivating them in West Virginia was a miracle; back home they grew only in the Red Sea.

Poor old Rem. Dragging his arthritic hips through the north wing, Abigail darting at his side, banging first into the china cabinet, then into the dining room table, no, old Rem was owed his due, was owed his remnants refuge.

Emopee was inspired again. To make his new book more conventional, he decided that it should be a straight historical novel. "Conventional stories are where the money is," Merriweather said to him in his evaluation. "One novel on the best-seller list and you'll be set for life," he said.

But was there a conventional novel in him, much less a straight historical novel? Something was in him, he knew. He concluded that the reason he was not successful with *The William Novel* was because, among other things, it had too much dialogue in it. By including more description this time, he'd have a better chance.

And so Constantinople at the height of the Byzantine Empire, 15th century A.D., was the setting for his new work, his conventional straight historical novel. Constantinople was a city on the Mediterranean, with trees full of bright green olives, and streams of dark water splashing down from the mountains all around. To these natural wonders he would add the man-made ones of the Hagia Sophia, that sprawling Christian church with its vast mosaics and vaulted ceilings, and Constantine's Forum with its shaft of porphyry topped with a gold cross. The Hippodrome, after Rome's Circus Maximus, he would have a field day with. From a book on the subject at Hick's Used Book Store he read that "high-powered political scandal, intrigue, brutality, mystery, and superstition were the order of the day there," everything, in short, that a writer of conventional novels needed.

The story's protagonist he decided would be a youth able, through mystical powers, to see the future, a talent generating its share of trouble for him, leading to the emperor himself. And as N. Emopee would be the one actually doing the seeing, with the help of that book at Hick's, it seemed rather a neat trick, he thought. The best would be the protagonist's prediction of the siege of Constantinople by the Turks in 1453 A.D., an attack resulting in the fall of the Byzantine Empire, which would be the novel's climax.

Settled on this plan, N. Emopee picked up a copy of agent Merriweather's own book on novels, which described literary devices of different kinds, plot twists and all that, detailing, at the same time, how to create unforgettable characters, in short how to write stories that will sell. Every syllable of advice that Mr. Merriweather recommended, he would include in his new novel, even if he longed for "two different realities occurring simultaneously, with events in the one affecting those in the other."

Longed for? Plato's Cave in Hick's Used Bookstore was once again suddenly a bonanza, theosophist Madame Blavatsky's two volume *The Secret Doctrine*, and her *Isis*

Unveiled topping his list of finds. Also on the shelf, "*The Bardo Thodol*," i.e. "*The Tibetan Book of the Dead*," edited by W. Y. Evans-Wentz, which described the Bardo Plane in the afterworld, and Madame Alexandra David-Neel's *With Mystics and Magicians in Tibet*.

Where, though, did all these books come from? Did one person sell them all to Mr. Hick, and if so, shouldn't he, N. Emopee, meet him or her, take tea with them? What a conversation they could have? The next time Mr. Hick was in the shop he would ask him.

That afternoon N. Emopee got a phone call from the chairman of the Oboe Department over at Westhill Community College. "I received your resume, Mr. Emopee," Dr. Hobcourt, cheerfully, "and I am quite impressed with you, especially since you've performed with my old friend Hieronymus Hup at Stiff Arm, to say nothing of your three years here in Westhill with our Embouchure Ensemble. Indeed, you were their artistic director, your resume said," that sentence suffering a coffee spill, unfortunately, but if he thought it said artistic director so be it.

"Hup and I teach a conducting seminar in the summertime, as you know, or may know, and otherwise I've known him for thirty years. When I called him this morning to tell him of your application to teach Third-Chair oboing here, he was pleased to hear it. He allowed as how there was no one better qualified than you to teach the Third Chair, save that is for Ray Blinovich." Blinovich played for the Beckley

Oboe Orchestra at Beckley College, an anti-war college in the southern part of the state.

"I apologize for my lack of teaching experience," N. Emopee, quickly, "but, you see--"

"A minor detail, my dear N. May I call you N.?"

"N, it is."

"What I propose is that you come over here and sign a contract with me right away, if it would not be an inconvenience for you."

A contract right away? "Can you tell me what the teaching load would be, before I make my decision? I'm a novelist part time, you see, and I was hoping for time to--"

"Not a problem, N. But I thought you had already made up your mind on teaching, the sorry state of that residence of yours, not to embarrass you, all over the evening news this summer. It rather looks like you need cash flow just now. But then that's your affair. My requirements are six courses per semester, not all that much really, not for you anyway, all the same course, *The Joys of Third Oboing*."

"And the pay? How much do I get paid for six courses?"

"Non-tenure track, of course, so I can only start you at $9,000 per year, which may not seem like much, but you won't be working in the summer remember, or maybe you will, but not for me. You say you are a writer, so this would give you time for your own work."

True enough.

"So it sounds like the perfect arrangement for you, if you ask me, and a good deal for me, too, with your reputation around town."

"Around town and around the country," N. Emopee could not resist.

"Did I hear your price just go up?"

"I should tell you, though, that television doesn't do justice to One Pound Down Street, making it look worse than it really is," not true, but N. Emopee was trying to not look so desperate. "But money for repairs up there is a high priority for me, no question. It's going to be a refuge one day, you know."

"You don't say. My son is refugee, since my wife and I disowned him."

Marge of Marginal Typing down in Fairfield had considerable experience, that screenplay of *Lawrence of Fairfield* among her credits. But N. Emopee worried that she was not suited for novels, long works for which a considerable attention span was required. Marge seemed to him to not have much of that in reserve. A giveaway was how, after they spoke for five minutes over lunch, she forgot who he was.

The most N. Emopee ever weighed in his life was 165 pounds, during his oboe studies at USC, not many calories burned holding a musical instrument. During his exile years in Erie, however, he maintained a reasonable 156 pounds. The exception was when he was in crisis, when he was seeing those young ladies, for instance, the stress of which burned him down to 152. Now, though, he was at 145 pounds, and still dropping, which was beginning to worry him.

His writing routine was in part to blame, sitting at his desk in his plaid living room all day long, so that he had no appetite. This was the reverse of his college days when, despite his sedentary life, he was a bottomless pit. His weight loss here made sense, however. Now when he did get hungry, he ate only vegetables--well, starches, fruits and vegetables--vegan that he was. Little wonder he was skinny.

On top of it, he went out and painted houses for four days a week, back with his uncle out of both of their desperations, the On Again/Off Again Painting Company Rufus' business may as well be named, thirty-two grueling hours each week, when they had it, with the result that he lost still more weight.

Not helping was his renovation of the house. While a stagehand and then a plumber in Pittsburgh, he acquired carpentry and mechanical skills. With his goal of changing his residence into a refuge, it was only natural that he would want to do some of the work himself. Even his bank manager liked the idea, a two-week reprieve from eviction.

As with *The William Novel*, his prospects for succeeding appeared rosiest in the period immediately following the submission of his work, this time the Constantinople story, titled *The Seer*, he sent it once more to Mr. Merriweather. Seeing the project to completion was certainly, once again, gratifying for him, despite the time it took him to finish it.

The hours, days, and weeks were agonizing, writing when he didn't feel like it, when everyone else was at parks or at restaurants or at the movies, or in bed, with only him alone at his work, all by himself, late into the night, witnessed by only him.

His adopted mother, meanwhile, knew when he had finished a project. He referred to it constantly, gobbling up what crumbs of praise she might have to offer him, for what it was worth, knowing that they were all he would get from her. Writing novels was at least better than oboing. Weren't there more novelists than oboists?

How in the world Eunice was ever attracted to Rem, much less was able to put up with him all those years, was forever, to N. Emopee, a monumental mystery. Then again it was because Rem was a teacher, probably. The world needed teachers, needed them almost as much as bus drivers, whom she favored as well. April, after all, was a teacher, and so should N. Emopee be when finally he got over this writing bit. Her one hope was that his stint at the Westhill Community College, coming up as it was in another week, would turn him around.

"Jiji muge is the unimpeded interpenetration of all things and events, much as every dew drop on a spider's web reflects every other dew drop. This means that everything that we do, and do not do, is reflected in everything around us." Ed was in the garage where he had lowered onto a stack of drop sheets he had placed on top of a wider pile of drop sheets. A zafu on top of a zabuton, by the look of them, and now sitting cross-legged there, a three-inch angular sash tool, like a lotus scepter, in his right hand, he looked positively saintly. "It is one thing to be ignorant of this, to simply not know it, and quite another to know it and to not act in accordance. Being ignore-ant, knowing something and ignoring it, is like driving a car with bald tires and pretending that they are not. Most people purposefully ignore most things in their lives."

"I'm with you," N. Emopee.

Rufus's resentment of his nephew manifested itself in peculiar ways, as when one afternoon they were working side by side on the overhang of a house in uptown Morganhill.

"Eunice showed me pictures that Rem took at your wedding, did I tell you?" N. Emopee, brightly, spontaneously, and well meaning.

Rufus, brisling, "Your dad's camera jammed. The pictures must have been taken by somebody else."

"How does Eunice have them then?"

"Whoever took them, gave her copies of them, obviously."

They got down from their stepladders and moved apart three feet.

"Joyce and I don't have any shots of the wedding ourselves, you know."

"Oh, I think you do," N. Emopee. "Aunt Joyce showed them to me last year."

"Is she keeping secrets from me again?" Rufus, a hoarse laugh.

They stepped down from their ladders and moved apart three more feet.

"Still, our wedding was quite an event I can tell you. Romantic, to put it mildly. We were high school sweethearts, you know."

"Were you?"

"It's had a good long run, wouldn't you say, forty-two years?"

"Rare these days," N. Emopee had to admit. "Rem and Eunice were married a long time, too, forty years."

"Eunice was swept off her feet by Rem, you know, poor thing."

Now Rufus had said this before, most recently on the occasion of Eunice's sixty-fifth birthday, and like previously, N. Emopee understood his insinuation. It was that Eunice was not in her right mind when she married Rem. Rem was not the most handsome man in the world, truth be told, not as good looking as Rufus, for instance, but didn't he make up for it in other ways? He was very caring.

"No, your mother was swept off her feet," Rufus once again, "poor dear."

Down from their ladders again, they moved to opposite ends of the house. "Yet," Rufus with a shout, "your dad and mother were married a long time, no question about it, a son and an adopted daughter, thirty-four and thirty-seven years old, respectively, to prove it."

N. Emopee, surprised his uncle remembered April's, much less his age, braced himself for a dig.

"Yeah, it was a big event when they adopted your sister. I remember it well. But not you, not to make you feel bad," even though it was. "Your parents didn't want you in the house," loud enough for their customer inside the house to hear.

Emopee marveled at how vicious Rufus, when he felt threatened, could be at times, the effect N. Emopee had on him for some reason. That evening N. Emopee wrote in his journal:

Even though he consciously makes his rude remarks, knows the effect that they have on me, feels satisfaction having made them, I still don't think he really means them. When I told Eunice what Rufus had said about Rem and her, about how he swept her off her feet, that she was not, in a word, in her right mind, and how they didn't want me in the house, she just laughed: 'Rufus shit! Rufus shit!' I would tell him what she said, except that it would only make things worse, feed the game, fuel the flames, when it is just sad. And besides, I need the work. After this last job, which had us on opposite ends of the house, wouldn't you know it, he gave me a raise.

Chapter Eleven
To Thine Own Self Be True

A sharp knock came to the teachers' lounge door at Westhill Community College, causing the book N. Emopee was reading, *Mysticism in the Modern Age*, to drop from his lap onto the floor. That he was jumpy just then was putting it mildly.

"Mr. Emopee?" a voice now to go with the rap.

N. Emopee stood abruptly and opened the door, the secretary looking all over for him she said.

"The students waiting for your lecture are about to leave."

N. Emopee stooped to pick up the book by the right leg of his chair. Losing himself in it had less to do with its contents, since he was already familiar with the subject from his past reading, than with the revelation by Mr. Hick that one person did indeed sell the bonanza N. Emopee had purchased the previous week. "They came from an estate," Hick told him, "the late Father Luthan Pool, a black Catholic priest who lived just up the hill here."

"You don't say," N. Emopee exclaimed. What more mystical religion than Catholicism, huh? But Madame Blavatsky's *The Secret Doctrine* and Evans-Wentz's interpretation of *The Bardo Thodol*, well, that's surely esoteric stuff, wouldn't you say, Mr. Hick, even for a Catholic priest? I'd love to have met him. In the next life, maybe."

But now embarrassed over this slip of his on his very first day at Westhill, his heart pounding heavily now in anticipation, or was it in dread, he stepped from the lounge and strode down to the front lobby. This building, the Creative Arts Center of Westhill, was where, coincidentally, he once performed with the Embouchure Ensemble, so that as he departed the lobby for the backstage area, he felt right at home.

However, on reaching the wings, where three more steps would have him onstage, he saw now that this was not the concert theatre where he had once oboed, but rather the drama theatre, what the concert theatre became when the great acoustical shell, the sides and ceiling, were retracted to the back wall. What remained was the dark gaping fly gallery overhead and the black vertical drapes, the velours, around the perimeter, every bit a cavern, to see it. It caused N. Emopee to shudder, all of a sudden. Still, the show must go on, he reminded himself, remembering that this was for all the remnants who would come to his refuge one day, to Rem's refuge. Out he stepped then to the lectern awaiting him, and to the students in rows the whole way up the auditorium.

"I almost didn't make it, did I?" a tug of air. The one hundred students stared back at him as though, like most students, they wished he hadn't, especially here at lunchtime on a warm autumn afternoon. Yet as Third-Chair oboists in training, they knew they needed this course before they could advance to the upper division classes, and so they all squirmed once, in unison, and settled in for the hour-long lecture.

"My name is Mr. Emopee, and I will be your professor for this semester, which is a survey of Third-Chair oboing from ancient to modern times, which, considering that the oboe did not exist in ancient times, at least not as an oboe, is no small feat," a joke by N. Emopee that went over like a lead parachute. These students, after all, being out of high school for no more than a month, did not expect humor from a professor, not from a new one certainly, the word out on N. Emopee. All the same, they did, as first-year college students always did, write in their notebooks every word, every syllable, even the joke that N. Emopee said.

N. Emopee stopped. The students' pens screeched to a halt at the same moment, the students looking up. For now, all of a sudden, N. Emopee was unable to speak. Clearing his throat to make everything all right again, hopefully, what the computer teachers in the lounge termed "rebooting to the default settings," he continued, or attempted to pick up where he left off. A second purging of his throat, punctuated by a cough, and he resumed.

But he did not resume. His mind, it seemed, had gone blank, leaving him to grab for his rumpled briefcase at his feet, from which emerged a stack of his oboing notes from his college days. He had studied them in their entirety for this class. Yet, as his eyes dug at the words therein, he realized that he might as well be looking at hieroglyphics.

"Pardon me, please," he mouthed, softly, whereupon he stepped back from the lectern and took a deep breath, a handkerchief wiping his beading brow.

What was happening here? Stage fright was not the matter. He had performed on this very stage, in fact on many such stages during his career as an oboist, albeit in their concert configurations, but this shouldn't make any difference. The students, all the while, looked on in bewilderment.

Back to the lectern, where his notes continued to read like a foreign language, he brought to mind once more, to inspire him, his refuge-to-be, capping it with the memory of Rem, who had said to him "Swear," even though recalling it only made things worse. As did his glance into the wings where he discovered Dr. Hobcourt watching him, perplexed, too.

In the end, he just stood there and wordlessly moved his mouth.

The envelope danced in N. Emopee's trembling hand. With a sigh, with a bold breath and a sigh, he tucked his oboic thumb through the top edge of the long manila envelope and peeled out the pages within.

"This is definitely more conventional writing, Mr. N. Emopee," the report from Mr. Merriweather began, positively. "I like that you've abandoned your quirkiness. However, let's get right to it, shall we? *The Seer*, while original enough, and written with flare and surprising polish for someone so new to the craft, is in trouble, however. The difficulty is that your protagonist doesn't really have a problem, the key to any novel's success. Sure 'Milo' has difficulties, and has them all the way to the emperor himself, but these, unfortunately, do not carry the work. All you've given me is a string of incidents, and incidents, as dramatic as they might be, do not constitute a story, not a saleable story.

"Your other failing is that your writing, while enthusiastic, reads like a police report, this happened, then that happened, then this happened, so that the story feels predigested, hence lifeless and unengaging.

"And, lastly, and most disastrously, you don't reveal enough about your protagonist for us to get close to him, close enough to care what happens to him. We feel less for the hero at the end than we do at the beginning, not an easy accomplishment at that. For these reasons I must decline representing *The Seer*. And while you may attempt a repair of it if you wish, my suggestion, as I've thought about it further, is that you chalk this one up to experience and move on. Your next novel I'm sure will be right on the mark. Good luck to you. Yours sincerely, Scott Merriweather."

It was the final nail in the coffin, or rather the nail was up and now struck. To keep it from sinking all the way in, N. Emopee immediately launched into that next novel Mr. Merriweather referred to, which kept him from feeling the rejection of this one for another full day, until at last the truth came home to him, and he broke down. No Emopee in family history had ever blubbered that much.

Months had passed since he undertook this attempt to get his life back on track, months of failure, of time wasted, of trying, first, to get into the biz as a story analyst, what he called "alternative oboing," but then as a screenwriter, where he learned more money was to be made. Still more money was to be had as a novelist, he read, hence his first book *The William Novel*, followed by *The Knower*. *The Knower*, however, he abandoned in favor or the more conventional *The Seer*. Yet to date he had nothing to show for all this, just rejection, astonishing for a man who seemed to have so much to offer, but who now was in ruin.

"Teaching is not who I am." N. Emopee trying to explain to Dr. Hobcourt his meltdown onstage.

"A lot of people are not who they are," Hobcourt.

"Plus, it's irrelevant."

"Everything's irrelevant, Mr. N. Emopee. Get over it."

"But with some things there's no middle ground. Regrettably, I'm learning this the hard way, and not just at my own expense."

"At your expense, sir. I'm suing you for breach of contract."

Which was when three letters from his stagehand pals back in Pittsburgh arrived in his mailbox, jar, friends who reported to him that they were now crew leaders and department managers, what <u>he</u> would have been, too, had he remained in the north. <u>They</u> were crew leaders and managers, while all he was, for all practical purposes, was a painter. Even Rufus was embarrassed for him.

If N. Emopee was none of all this, though, what was he? Possibly he was a monk after all, what typist Emily saw in him. He should just head off to a monastery and get it over with.

But he was not, like Father Pool, a Catholic, or a member of any organized religion. He had an intellectual interest in organized religion, but would never become a member of one. No, it rather seemed if he was to be a monk, he would have to be one by himself, a "lone rhino on the plain," as a wandering monk, one not in a monastery, was called in Buddhism. He would be his own monastery.

But that wasn't it either.

Alas, he now knew what he was.

"Is there anything I can get for you upstream, Nathan?"

Cleo was bobbing in her bird's-nest-size, crow's-nest-size canoe, at her side a five-foot stick of driftwood, birch it looked like, to be her oar.

What relatives she had upriver to visit, what this was all about supposedly, was anyone's guess, likely none whatsoever. This was the same as her attempt to hitchhike on the Morganhill freeway that time, except that this time there was no antidote, no Flee-Aid in this case. So he had to let her go.

He could alert the local mental health agency, which surely would pack her away in an institution, which in his affection for her, one eccentric to another, he did not want to see happen. At the same time he worried that all this was his fault, the east wing shower that she had come to rely on having collapsed that past Friday. The wood and nails he scavenged from it for his renovations elsewhere in the house having weakened it. "How about the west wing shower?" to her, subsequently, but her mind was made up.

"Toodaloo, Nathan," and she was away, her bag of crow bones still slung on her back.

As for where Cleo was headed exactly, the air conditioner run-off down the concrete-lined Missing River would get her, if she was lucky, to the city of Azusa, home of John Phillip Azusa, the bandmaster, or a bandmaster, often confused with the other guy. From Azusa on, it would be hiking the dry river bed into the Hollywoods Hills, formerly Cooper's

Rock State Forest, which Cleo was unlikely to do, given her fear of bears.

The only thing that would stop her now, as N. Emopee waved a desperate farewell to her, would be a change in the weather. The end of the hot spell would mean an end to the air-conditioner trickle, which would have her canoe dead in the water soon enough, dead in the concrete. Only Ed, of his circle of friends, if Ed and Cleo formed a circle, remained, and he, Ed, had one foot out the door, too, being paid one brush full at a time now. Then, Ed was more an employee than a friend, not unlike N. Emopee's relatives, his aunts and uncles, whom he scarcely knew. He considered them associates more than friends. Not even his sister April, born in May, was a friend, so much as the family foreman. He breathed a despairing sigh.

N. Emopee had a bad feeling about the Missing River on which Cleo was now embarked, because he knew now how she would fare on it. And he knew how he knew.

The Missing River was missing until it was found, which was to say that once it was found it was recognizably no longer missing. Not always missing, it was once the sturdy Monongahela River, except that Hollywoods, in their filming of *Lawrence of Fairfield*, needed a desert, and a desert did not have a river running through it. Their solution was to squeeze off the river at the dam down at Fairfield, two years ago now that was, to reduce the flow.

With the river from Fairfield to Morganhill but a memory now, the dilemma then became what to do with the gully, the trench, the ditch left behind. Calvin Crump, N. Emopee's old producer acquaintance, "King of 'B' Movies," had the "B" solution. With no opposition, save for the odd catfish still on the river bed, he sent in a fleet of cement trucks. The result was that the bottom and banks of the river, for as far as the eye could see, were quickly as solid as rock. All the transplanted biz types were nostalgic, if not down right homesick at the sight of it. It reminded them of the Los Angeles River back in L.A., also a concrete canal

But what of property values for the cottages along the Missing river? They plummeted with the plummeting water, of course. The Public Broadcasting System, PBS, though, knowing everything about everything, was quick to the rescue. Setting their annual fund drive in the trench, the "pledge trench" they called it, they produced the Three Tenors, twelve Julia Child cooking shows, and a Donnie Osmond concert, with the white walls of the cement as the backdrop.

OBC, then, in a remake of the Steve McQueen movie *Bullitt*, put a car chase through the gully, the whole town turning out to watch. By month's end, the sport of handball, making use of the walls, caught on, as did skateboarding up and down the walls and floor. The U.S. Olympic track team trained there in June, whereupon the property values again skyrocketed, indeed tripled in worth, the price of front row seats.

"Please give me more time."

"Time?" This was Mr. Snover, Thor Snover the bank manager at Morganhill City Bank. That this very same morning the architect's drawings for Mickey Mountain should arrive, for the bank's approval, for financing, was a coincidence indeed. "Too late for you, Mr. Emopee," a scrunch of Snover's short nose and a pursing of his thin lips. "You see, I've padlocked your gates today. There's no getting in for you any longer. Try to enter and my security guard Ed will have with you."

Ed? Buddhist Ed?

"You've never had assets seized before have you?" Snover added. "Have you thought of getting a lawyer?"

He had indeed thought of getting a lawyer, and had one, Mr. Hestormantle, even sending him to the bank, but a lot of good that did him.

N. Emopee dashed home to try Ed, except that Ed wouldn't let him in the gate.

"You won't what?"

Ed stood silently in his crisp new security guard uniform, a stone Buddha to see him.

"Okay, I'll let you paint the whole exterior of the house," except that there was no exterior of the house left.

Ed looked in a meditation of some sort, face flat, eyes blankly into space.

"Okay, you don't have to actually unlock the gate. Just let me borrow the key for a minute. What I do with it is my own business kind of thing." You'd think N. Emopee worked for the government.

N. Emopee, it turned out, spent the night at Cleo's camp down over the hill, accessible from the lower road, certain that she would not object to it, miles away as she was by now. It gave him a roof over his head at least, or a tarpaulin over it. His wine cellar was his first choice, but it had caved in the week before, all those cases of pomegranate port he finally auctioned off at a pittance all that was holding the place up.

"So then--ouch." He had just plopped onto Cleo's salvaged La-Z-Boy lounge chair, a lazy spring giving him a good poke. "Cleo's fairwell," his hands in the air; he glared at the chair. He reached over and clicked on the TV, the coat hanger rabbit ears quivering once, which then provided him, ever so slowly, a black and white image of the dwarf Tattoo on *Fantasy Island*, "Da plane, da plane," in the all too familiar dockside scene. This was the new, leaner, meaner *Fantasy Island*, though, filmed up at the lagoon at the Morganhill Arboretum. This was the same lagoon, in fact, with all its water fowl, "Da ducks, da ducks," that N. Emopee continued, until recently, to visit on the third Tuesday of every month, free admission day, for walking meditation. However, he wasn't in the mood for Tattoo just now, alas, but since it was the only channel he could find down there in the grove, he just shut the thing off.

Satisfying his hunger, not having eaten all day, would be a substitute entertainment for him he decided, so he rummaged through Cleo's refrigerator, teetering as it was beside a nearby pomegranate tree, wasn't the tarpaulin getting pelted by the fruit as he stood there, or was it greetings from all the crows overhead.

These crows proved more in Cleo's routine than she had told him about. He saw now what she did when one got within range. If he read the labels in the freezer correctly, here was crow coq au vin, crow croquettes, and crepes a la crow, to name just three, even crowcaroni and cheese, a fourth. "When in Rome--" N. Emopee finally. He went for the crowcaroni and cheese.

With a mighty yawn then, he decided to call it a night, settling onto the sofa across the way, by the laurel bush. Only one of the three long cushions was the least bit worn he noticed, the extent of the sofa Cleo took up. However no sooner was he fast asleep than he was fast awake again, an odd moaning from up at the mansion. His heart pounded wildly at the sound. But then as it repeated, this time in sing-song fashion, he relaxed, recognizing Ed singing the Zen sutra "Hokekyo."

N. Emopee switched on Cleo's TV set again, to check the weather, but *Fantasy Island* was still on, and that wasn't going to do him any good. But what was this? Where the dwarf Tattoo had stood, the dwarf Cleo now laid, peering coldly from the pier of the show's set at the arboretum. She had just washed into the lagoon from a disaster on the Missing River, according to the police officer being interviewed on the scene. "What we have here is a drowning."

"A drowning!" N. Emopee's outburst woke the crows in the rookery overhead, a loud squawk from them in reply.

"An investigation is underway," the policeman, in conclusion.

But then a traffic helicopter pilot chimed in, having seen it all happen, all about how the lady's canoe collided with a washing machine discarded in the river at the bridge in Point Marion. The good news, she went down in only five feet of water, the bad news, she was only four feet six inches tall.

How N. Emopee knew this was going to happen, or something like it, he did not know. Except that he did know.

Ed, after one week as a rent-a-cop, had returned to his Zen center, the Ohio Eyes Zen Center, over on the Ohio River below New Martinsville, fifty-five miles to the west. He had been promoted to abbot there, it so happened. But he did not depart One Pound Down Street without a final observation for N. Emopee, as stated in a letter he left in the mason jar mailbox at the house's front doorstep, what was left of it.

N. Emopee struggled to open the jar, the heat of the day making it too hot to hold for long, where he read, "Whatever teachings of the Buddha there may be, you can assure yourself, N. Emopee, that they conduce to dispassion, and not to passions; to detachment and not to bondage;

to decrease of worldly gains, and not to their increase; to frugality and not to covetousness; to content and not to discontent; to solitude and not to company; to energy and not to sluggishness; to delight in good and not to delight in evil; of such teachings, N. Emopee, you may with certainty affirm: This is the Norm. This is the Discipline. This is the Master's Message.

"As I leave you today I ask you one favor," Ed continued. "Forgive me for not letting you through your gate this past week. I was only doing the job I was hired to do, to make a dollar or two for the Ohio Eyes Zen Center. Know, at the same time, that your presence down at Cleo's camp was known to me all along, but that I told no one about it. You had, at least, a shelter for the night, of which I was glad. Good luck to you and farewell."

Men did not know how to be friends with other men except to compete with them, but N. Emopee never felt that he and Ed were ever in competition. They had nothing to compete about. They were both shadows.

And so, minus Cleo and Ed, his circle of friends was now down to a dot, himself, and he wasn't on the best of terms with himself currently. Still, in the end, he felt that he was better off this way. "Be a refuge onto yourself," the Buddha taught, even if for N. Emopee it was only the half of it. There was another half of him now.

It occurred to N. Emopee that he might be a Buddhist mystic, even though there was no such thing really. A person was either a Buddhist or he was a mystic. A Buddhist held that everything other than following the Buddha's path to ending suffering in the world was irrelevant, while a mystic argued that everything other than union with the Godhead was beside the point.

But they were not mutually exclusive groups. Buddhism was atheistic, although Buddhists believed that higher levels of consciousness were mystical, or approached mysticism. Mysticism was not atheistic. Joining with the Godhead was its priority.

But mystics were also human, hence suffering was concern of theirs as well. You could not unite with the Godhead if you had a migraine headache, for instance. A migraine headache also kept a Buddhist from reaching greater levels of consciousness.

Was N. Emopee a Buddhist mystic then? No. He was something else altogether.

The following day Eunice died. Apparently she had taken two aspirin for it, whatever it was, hoping it would go away, except that she went away instead. N. Emopee was stunned. His tears, though, when at last they came, were not painful for him so much as a relief, a surprise relief even, for they made him feel human for the first time in a year.

If he was critical of Eunice at all, it was because she was critical of him, during the beginning of the year in particular. She didn't go to all the trouble of giving birth to him just to have him fail, she told him. But then she came around later in the year and was one of his most ardent supporters. Mothers were like this.

In the meanwhile, N. Emopee was still painting with his uncle, albeit two not four days per week, an arrangement negotiated by him with considerable resistance from Rufus, who would lose money in the deal. N. Emopee's argument was that he needed more time for his writing, when really the fewer days were so he wouldn't feel like only a painter again. It was a psychological thing for him, all about his keeping his morale up during this time of crisis.

It was, at the same time, a risk. Less income from painting meant that the number of tours he was conducting at the mansion had to increase. However, to get more tourists he had to advertise in the local newspaper, but with no money to advertise, he was left to posting signs on neighboring roads. Which was when, as he learned subsequently, a city ordinance prohibited signs by private citizens along any of the city's streets, and so down his signs came within minutes of their going up.

The other half of the problem was that there was nothing left to tour at the house, really. His renovation of the front of the house was at the expense of the rest of it, so that there was precious little left for anyone to see any longer.

Only two days of painting per week with his uncle was also because Rufus was making rude remarks to him once more, this time about N. Emopee's loss of that teaching job over at Westhill Community College, which he saw as final evidence, once and for all, that his nephew was a loser.

Chapter Twelve
Stuart Stair Incident

*D*ue to these latest grim developments, N. Emopee decided to immerse himself more fully in mysticism, walking meditation in the Hollywoods Hills, jogging meditation in the Missing River, and television meditation in Cleo's camp. As for his writing, well, he was head long into it again, despite himself, not a novel this time, but more poetry. Poetry made him feel closer to what he really was.

But now was this poetry "regression," to use the psychological term for it, a return to a behavior which in the past made him feel happy? He felt better for it, whatever the case. Whatever worked.

To make ends meet, N. Emopee phoned Homer Tank at OBC to see whether, on the off chance, Tank might give him another shot at free-lance story analysis, analyzing scripts for film and television. The difference this time was that it had nothing to do with a career for him, but only for a few extra dollars. Of course there was not much to be had from reading in the best of times, but every little bit helped.

As it happened, a changing of the guard had occurred in his absence, Tank retiring finally. The department was run now by one Tiller Mills, one of the senior readers there, whom Tank had mentioned to him, not by name, but who was one of his regulars.

"Sure, N., I can give you work," the result of a sympathetic scan of N. Emopee's coverages on file in the front office. "We'll want to consider you for the director's position as well, if you're interested."

"Me?"

"We've always been partial to oboists. Call me again next week."

And as if this were not good news enough, his mason jar contained a response to an application he submitted three months earlier. It informed him that he was a finalist for the chairman of the Third-Chair Oboing department at the newly-opened Hollywoods University down on Ritchie Bordeaux Way.

"In addition to administration," which N. Emopee had no experience doing, although he'd be administering only himself the letter said, a one-person department, "you will also team-teach, along with Ms. Hooter Newton of the Comedy department. This course would be *"From Biz Kids to Biz Brats: the Pitfalls and Pratfalls of Third-Chair Oboing,"* which to N. Emopee had straight man to Ms. Newton written all over it. "Still, good news, I have to say," the interview to take place in two more days.

But what about Hobcourt over at Westhill Community College? Wasn't he suing him for breach of contract? They would never hire him at Hollywoods University if they got wind of the suit. Fearing that it might still happen, N. Emopee promptly phoned Hobcourt and asked him point blank, "Are you still suing me?"

"Did I say I was suing you?"

"You're a writer, I understand."

N. Emopee glanced at the image alongside his in the wall-to-wall mirror of the crowded men's locker room at the Palace of Pump gym, where he had come to work off his jitters before the interview at Hollywoods University. "Who told you that?"

"You did, I guess," the man confessing at the end. "I overheard you talking about it to another gentleman the other day."

"A long while ago because I haven't been a writer for a month at least."

"Possibly, yes, it might have been some time ago," the inquirer's canvas gym bag from his left hand to his right, his soft slacks and bulky knit sweater getting a tug. "My students read a lot of writers in the courses I teach, is why I asked. I thought you might be one they were reading currently."

"Do they? Do you? Me?" N. Emopee pulled a comb through his thinning hair, not sure what to make of this man.

"I'm the director of the scholars program where I teach," the man finishing. "The name is Wishborn Corbette. You can call be Bob."

"Hi, Bob."

"In fact, in two of my scholars program courses, *'What Is Existence?'* and *'What Are Human Beings?'*" presumptuous of him it seemed to N. Emopee, "we read thirty writers in each course."

"That's a lot." N. Emopee didn't know where this was leading, not quite, not yet.

"What do you write, if you don't mind my asking?" Bob.

"Well, novels more recently, Maeterlinckian," even though Maeterlinck never wrote a novel, but, "you get the idea. Mystical. Back, that is, when I was still writing novels. Just a few poems now."

"A hard way to make a living, poems."

The two of them started for the front lobby, but not before N. Emopee remarked, "my poems are not for making me a living. They're a spiritual thing. As for your next question, no, I've never had anything published."

"How do you survive then? Everything costs money these days."

Bob was getting awfully personal all of a sudden, the nerves N. Emopee had just worn off, back on.

"Survive?" N. Emopee, sharply. "There are lots of ways to survive. You have some Ihaven't thought of, perhaps."

Bob drew back.

N. Emopee sighed. "I was supposed to teach over at Westhill Community College this year, but it didn't work out."

"Oh, good. Or rather, sorry to hear it." The word "good" was a Freudian slip. Bob did not buy that this guy was qualified to teach anything, or even ever a writer, for that matter.

In the parking lot, they stopped for a final farewell, for this day at least, until, "Say," said Bob. "I never did get your name."

Unaccustomed to giving it out without a resume, N. Emopee fussed, only to stick out his hand. "N. Emopee is my name."

Bob stared. "Not <u>the</u> N. Emopee, surely," forgetting that, with a name like that, the odds were slim of any others.

"That's me."

"You're the guy with the big house up on the hill. I've heard about you on the news. You're converting it to a refuge for remnants of foreign wars, I read."

Naturally, he wouldn't know the extent to which the refuge was N. Emopee's sworn duty, derailed though it was at the moment, possibly forever, but so be it for now.

"You would also be the N. Emopee who protested the Hayfields and McCays war nine years ago. You were in the news for that, too."

"They're afraid of me you know, the Hayfields and McCays."

"Except that they tossed you out of the state. Both families. Erie, P.A. is where you wound up, it was reported."

"You have a good memory."

"Only with a new governor, Zelda Dilworth, could you get back here, a pardon I believe it was; am I right?"

N. Emopee buttoned his jacket for his wait at the bus stop across the street, no longer using his blimp-of-a-station wagon these days, to save money. "Nine years ago we had a pro-war governor in Hackett, pro-war because he was making money hand over glove off the Hayfields and McCays, off that latest dustup of theirs, t-shirts, plates, pennants. They were all in cahoots. And it's not the end of it, you'll see."

"If history is any evidence, you're right."

Everyone who was anyone, and some who weren't, like Rufus, were at Eunice's funeral. Even Eunice was there, and on time for once. Yet for N. Emopee it was depressing more than he expected. It was because Eunice did not look right to him, there on display amid all the flowers. Always when there was company, she would say, "Let me put my face on," by which she meant her makeup, but by which N. Emopee took to mean her social face, her egoic self. But now here at her funeral her face, her makeup, was put on by someone other than her, by a funeral cosmetic engineer, or whatever the title was, so that Eunice, as everyone agreed, looked less like herself than Mussolini. Yet N. Emopee was not now going to tell technician to put this eyebrow here and that one there, and that, no, they shouldn't be as thick as that, Eunice not having eyebrows to begin with.

On the other hand, the funeral, as Eunice understood, was only a twenty-minute deal, followed by her thank you, were she still alive, to everyone for coming, and that she hoped the punch was okay, "On to the ash heap, shall we?" She just would have wanted it to be over with.

Ash heap? Rem began the tradition, cremation the way to go, not really an ash heap, well, yes, an ash heap, the memorial grounds around the church where the service was held. For Rem it was out to sea. For N. Emopee it would be the Missing River when it was not missing.

"Eunice never wanted to stand out in a crowd," N. Emopee, one last look at her eyebrows. "Too late."

As N. Emopee stepped out of the church, a neighbor of Eunice's, Baxter Sleet, pulled him aside. He wanted to tell him that he had just sold his house, and that he was moving south, heading for his roots in Monroe County, where his ancestors had fought during the Civil War. They had not fought in the Civil War, only during it, and among themselves, but it was not his point. He wanted to get away and start fresh, he said, make something of his retirement. Opening a taco stand, he was thinking. He liked tacos, he said. He was saying it to make N. Emopee feel bad, like he, N. Emopee, should open a taco stand, too, or at least this was how it felt.

"When are you coming up to visit us?" meanwhile. This was April, now strolling alongside N. Emopee outside the church.

"Us?"

"I'm married now, didn't I tell you?"

"Well, no, I don't think you did, although maybe you did. Did you? No, it was Eunice who told me you were married."

"I'm married with three kids."

"Three kids? All at once?"

"No, my daughter Skippi was first, followed fast on her heals, so to say, by the twins."

That, according to N. Emopee's calculations, would be fifteen, counting April's children by her previous two marriages, reproductive biology her specialty at her school, little wonder.

Meantime, April, no small presence at 6'3" and 150 pounds, was accustomed to having her way with her kid brother, the 5'10," 130-pound N. Emopee, and so she repeated, "When are you coming up to visit?"

N. Emopee held his ground this time, though, putting it frankly, "For what purpose, April? Would there be a reason for it?"

It was a good question, complicated, five full minutes for April to digest it, at the end of which they just shook hands and left in separate cabs. Sad.

The West Virginia and Regional Archives contained a local man's personal letters written during his training as a medic for the latest, nine years ago now, Hayfields and McCays war, and which N. Emopee needed to research for his article about his opposition to this same war for *The Yorker* magazine. Bob had suggested it. This young man, Stuart Stair, after coming to oppose the war, was killed one month into it, sending a shock wave through the whole community. His friends and family were especially grieved since they believed, to a person, that he, a good soul, would prevail over ANY adversity in his life, even war. To this day a grief hung heavily in the valley, a sorrow that N. Emopee would describe in his piece, to be entitled "Was it Worth It?" The war's folly would be the theme.

However, what began as a one-hour session in front of the microfilm reading machine at the Archives turned into four hours, as N. Emopee could not free himself from the compelling letters, which for N. Emopee brought Stair back to life.

Brought him back to life? At the height of N. Emopee's involvement in the letters, a storm erupted outside, burst out of nowhere, a fury streaking from the mountains, as though born of them, down into the valley. With it the blinds in the reading room whipped and crashed, water poured in at every opening, and the overhead lights flashed on and off. Fearing that the viewing screen would explode, he switched the reading machine off, whereupon the storm vanished just as suddenly as it appeared.

Was this a coincidence? Then, what was he to make of the front page of the local newspaper, the *Morganhill Dominion-Post*, the very next morning, where there was a whole story about Stuart, along with a big picture of him there on the front page. Nine years had past since Stuart was killed, and now this.

What was unsettling about it was that he, N. Emopee, had caused it.

Thor Snover, the bank manager, had replaced Ed at the front gate with an electronic surveillance camera, three of them as a matter of fact, meaning that the house remained off limits for N. Emopee. It was just him and the crows, the only living things around there, N. Emopee still able, barely able, to sneak into Cleo's camp. Remaining on his mind the Stuart Stair incident at the library the day before, the sudden storm, and then the feature in the local newspaper, both of which were out of the blue. It was a favorable sign, he concluded, for that article of his about war and, should the war start again, the need to oppose it. The piece was to be his own story, mainly, including his exile in Erie, but it could just as well be that of any of the anti-warriors in the region.

If he was inspired, words for the article flowing from him like rain, it included his plans for his new remnants refuge, back on the front burner for him. Actually, they were not his plans but Rem's, Rem's blueprints, which he had laid out down at Cleo's camp this time. Already he had a full page of notes concerning the décor, which like his article would have a theme. "Salvation," he would make it, reflecting not only the saving of the stranded foreign wars remnants, but also the saving, the rescue, of his house, virtually only a memory now. "I'll rebuild," he promised himself once again, this time out loud. "Mickey Mountain over my dead body."

His salvation theme would include fabric on the walls with colorful images painted on them, oceans and forests and other calming images. And lots of natural lighting, skylights and the like. And music. He'd have a sound system designed just for oboe music. He recalled, for example, Debussy's *Les Oboiques.*

At the bamboo post holding up the tarpaulin beside him, a brown spider stood pondering him at length, whereupon it dropped all the way down to the bottom, only to then scamper the whole distance up to the top again, not unlike his own fortunes these days, he could only think. Meantime, the smell of the damp earth, the pungency of the rotting leaves, he found relaxed him, even as it felt like a grave to him. Still a vegan, he poked at the crow casserole, one of Cleo's, the meat out and to the side. His coke-bottle glasses got a shove and his now long hair a swipe with his arthritic fingers. He knew now that he would prevail here in the end, somehow would get through it all.

Having been down this road before, he braced himself for the decision by *The Yorker* magazine regarding his antiwar article "Was it Worth It?" Submitting it over the transom, as it was called, unsolicited, he knew his odds weren't the best. Rotating the envelope slowly, he took a tight tug of air, then a second calmer one, followed by a third one of shameless victory. Because contained within this envelope was his future. If the article was accepted for publication, it cleared the way for a book by him on the same subject, the proceeds from which would save his house, or at least the property, and the refuge could proceed.

Snap went the seal of the envelope and he lifted, confidently, the letter from its groove.

"Thank you for thinking of us, Mr. Emopee." This was Hazel Vent, the editor of *The Yorker* magazine. "West Virginia's Hayfields and McCays war has been a stone in our throats, too, and we have published ten studies of it in the past. Yet, despite our sympathies with you, this kind of autobiographical material, I'm sorry to say, is not suited for us."

N. Emopee groaned, sighed and then groaned again, even though it did not surprise him.

"The Hayfields and McCays war was not and is not a study," he dashed a letter back to Ms. Vent. "It has recurred these many decades precisely because all anyone does is study it. Personal material like mine is what will end the war once and for all. Please reconsider."

"We are sorry, Mr. Emopee," came a letter quickly in return, "but we still cannot use 'Was It Worth It?'"

Professor Bob, Wishborn Corbette late for his class *"What Are Human Beings?"* just said "Oh," although clearly he was disappointed, too. He after all was the one who had suggested the article to him.

A dreary rainy day in Morganhill found N. Emopee still camped out in Cleo's camp, where he was lamenting the loss of the house, and his wine cellar, now just a hole in the hill under the steps leading to the pomegranate grove. His shoulder rested against the old Kelvinator refrigerator Cleo had salvaged from a Salvation Army rejection bin. He was bemoaning, most of all, the fact that he was so cold here in the grove, recalling how a short year earlier he was all dry and toasty in his plaid living room up on the hill, now a pile of lumber sold at auction down in town. The house was built entirely of mahogany, mahogany studs, mahogany joists, mahogany floors, fetching a fortune, he suspected, but not for him. The bank was the one whose bonanza this was.

Whether that period of prosperity in his life was really worthwhile, and whether the simple life he was living now wasn't entirely better, wasn't less corrupting, less distracting for him, he was left now to consider. "I think it is better," the best face he could put on it. It didn't change the fact that he was still cold as hell.

Which was when the letter carrier came trudging through the grove, blunt brown boots kicking through the fallen leaves and coming to a stop front and center in front of him.

"Come in, come in," N. Emopee, brightly, as cheerfully as he could manage.

"Come in where?" the letter carrier, unavoidably, and who was mourning still the loss of the mason jar up at the house, sold to the highest bidder, too, a nuisance to hike all the way down here to the camp. Even so, neither rain, nor snow, etc. It was just lucky the carrier was willing to sneak in, under the surveillance cameras, and dogs now too.

"A postcard for you, Mr. Emopee, not much more, a coupon, and an ad for *The Yorker* magazine."

"Thanks, Gus, may I call you Gus?"

"I'd rather you call me Marilyn," which as a woman she was entitled to, hard to tell these days with the uniforms and hair so much alike. N. Emopee glanced to see who the postcard was from, Marilyn on the edge of her boots, curious to know as well.

"My, my, my," N. Emopee with a gasp, John Phillip Azusa on the front, postmarked from Azusa the city, and signed by Cleo. "Cleo?!" he choked.

"Cleo?" Marilyn knew the story from the *Morganhill Dominion-Post* and was as perplexed now as N. Emopee, who had seen for himself Cleo's dead eyes on TV.

A closer look at the postmark, however, revealed that the card was sent just prior to Cleo's demise, immediately, ten minutes perhaps before she washed ashore there at the Morganhill Arboretum, in the lagoon there. She had mailed the card and then promptly had her catastrophe, her canoe a head-on collision with that washing machine, a Maytag, in

Point Marion. The timing of it was more than N. Emopee could bear. "Poor Cleo, my poor Cleo," he began to sputter.

Now, though, he spotted a message on the card, just one line, but how apt it seemed, as if Cleo was telepathic there at the end. "It's only a house, Nathan," the message simply in its entirety read, which in light of N. Emopee's lamenting that morning the loss of the house, felt now right on the mark to him. Because to be honest he also felt a great burden lifted from his shoulders with the development, a great mahogany burden raised, and quite frankly he didn't--no, he did, he missed the place, but, after all was said and done, it might be for the better. He missed it enough, though, to guarantee its return, was the point, not for his own sake but for the purpose it was intended in the first place, for Rem's intention. "Swear," to himself this time. "The refuge will be even better now that I'm starting from scratch. Swear or be damned."

Prakeyestrainriti, the candle-concentration exercise in raja yoga, was to discipline the mind, to teach it to remain focused on a single point for an extended period of time, 30 minutes, for instance. The first part of the exercise was simply to fix one's gaze on the flame of a candle, holding it in the attention for as long as possible without letting the mind wander.

But it was the second part that was so fascinating to N. Emopee and which here again this evening had him on the linoleum floor of Cleo's camp, the candle flickering intensely before him, a mere arm's length away. And brilliant the light was, too, against the black surroundings, once the single bulb in the camp was extinguished.

Next, after gazing at the flame for a full three minutes, he then, as his raja yoga book instructed him, cupped his hands over his eyes. Looking into the darkness there, he watched for the after-image to appear. And once in sight, as it came here again this night, he kept it in his view for as long as he practically could. He maintained it steadily in the center of his vision, not letting it drift, for ten full minutes, before it waned. Then as it receded, faded from his sight, he brought it back for another five complete minutes, quite an accomplishment for him at that.

He was practicing this exercise with great intensity just before his bedtime, in part to improve his concentration, although as a Third-Chair oboist, albeit a former one, he was focused already. The other part was to relax him, stress getting the better of him, given all that had been happening to him. So concentrated and relaxed was he in fact that often he simply keeled over right in place, sleeping like a baby there on the linoleum the whole night long.

But now as he concluded this latest session, there was this: The after-image in his cupped hands, sharp to his view only at the start usually, remained so even as it shrunk and receded into the distance of his distance vision.

Of his distance vision? He started.

Again he stared at the candle flame for three minutes, his hands back over his eyes promptly, the after-image just as suddenly back to view, and just as well defined, where he watched as in the next three minutes it receded. Yet just as the time before, it did not blur or in any way turn fuzzy as in the past. Rather it remained as crisp as a new-born child would see it. Was this what he thought it was? Could this possibly be?

His hands to his face once more, he now moved the candle farther along the linoleum, farther away, and then still farther away from him, until at the finish it was a full thirty feet across the floor.

"Hallelujah!" N. Emopee shrieked, shouted there in the heavy darkness, where the flame remained crystal clear, sharp as a pin. His failed distance vision was failing him no longer. "Miraculous," these same eyes welling up in joy. With his two ring fingers straightened, a yoga for them, too, possibly, if he could find out how to do it, he'd be back in business again, once more in the oboing trade, all his problems solved!

Chapter Thirteen
Spiritual Family

"Oh, hi, N. Good to hear your voice again," Tiller Mills of the OBC story department said.

"Likewise I'm sure." He had just given OBC that buzz, this being that week later, on the off chance that they had that fresh series of assignments for him, giving him much, sort of, needed cash. His comeback needed cash.

"You are phoning about getting some reading work, I assume."

"Yes, sir," the directorship, Tank's old job, still in the air as well he hoped. "By the way, my eyesight is 20/20 again. I won't explain how, but I wanted to tell you this straight away," forgetting that he had not told Mills about his eyesight to start with, that there was a problem with it, anymore than, "the ring fingers are still a bit stiff, hard for me to type, not enough however to keep me from working for you. You see, I have a new typing service, Marge Finch of Marginal Typing down in Fairfield. You may have heard of her. She typed *Lawrence of Fairfield.* So my coverages for you will look first rate."

"I'm sure they will, or would, N.," a quick sigh from Mills, "were it not for one small problem." Mills could hear over the phone N. Emopee's brow drop.

"A problem?"

"When I told them I was hiring you back, the programming department sent me an urgent memo."

"A memo? Urgent?"

Mills shrugged. "A business issue I'm afraid, N., whether we like oboists in this office or not. You see, we paid dearly the last time you were here, lost our shirts to put it another way."

This was news to N. Emopee. "It's news to me," he said.

"The head honcho in the programming department read your last coverage himself. It was brought to his attention after an underling did not like your 'take' on the property, a book he said it was."

"*The Evil in Me,* or something like that, as I remember," N. Emopee.

"You said in the coverage that you did not feel that such a purveyor of hate, as you called him, deserved a made-for-TV movie about him, didn't merit that kind of attention. You said that Kettle, the author, would lap it up and do it even more."

"I said this, yes."

"Except that we don't pay our analysts for these kinds of opinions, N. It's not your job to do so. Whether or not a story would make compelling viewing for our audience, based on the guidelines we gave you, is all we want from you."

"But Kettle is a scum bag."

"As it happened, your coverage caused this same underling to hesitate before saying anything about it, delaying by one day the decision whether or not to go forward with the story. Consequently our competitor, BBS, the Better Broadcasting System, beat us to the punch, had the TV-movie on the air a day ahead of us. As a result we lost money, N., mega bucks."

"Because of me?"

"The kiss of death for you, N. Sorry."

"That I no longer own One Pound Down Street," he wrote in his journal, "that an empty lot is all that remains of it, and that I still am trespassing down here in Cleo's camp, does not concern me. Trespassing? The bank manager, Thor Snover, hasn't been here in a month, not since the would-be new owner, prospective buyer Harley Tickett, backed out of the Mickey Mountain deal. Beyond those three surveillance cameras at the front gate, Snover doesn't have any security here at all. There's nothing left to secure. Last night, in fact, I hauled my Mason jar mailbox, a new one, back up to the road."

Which was when an odd feeling came over him, the sense of being alone suddenly, but more so than he'd felt it in the past. The feeling was that something was absent from the scene. Fidgeting in the stark silence--the stark silence? This surely was it. For gone was the omnipresent squawk, gurgle, and clicking of the crows high in their rookery outside. N. Emopee, out from under the tarpaulin now, shown a flashlight skyward.

It was stunning. There was, it happened, not a crow to be seen in any direction, least of all up. But what did this mean? Had his creditors taken the crows with them, too? Were his prized pomegranate trees the next to go?

Yet no sooner was he outraged at this thought than he was overcome by the notion that this was "sign" to him. This was something speaking to him, loudly and clearly. He must prepare himself.

Hatha Yoga for the Arthritic Ring Fingers of Former Oboists was his latest, most timely find at Hick's Used Bookstore. Information there, coupled with his improved eyesight, would change everything.

His ring fingers out on the linoleum floor at Cleo's camp, N. Emopee began with the famous, according to the book, cobra exercise, less like a snake than a cat stretching its back backwards. If the ring fingers bulked at this, it was because they weren't designed for such an odd maneuver, or so they would argue if they could, except that by the end of it, they rather seemed to like it. As they also liked the plough, the locust, and, at the finish, the bow. They enjoyed them so much, as a matter of fact, that they told their neighbors, contagion being what it was, so that by the next day all ten fingers were in the act. All of them were moving in unison like a class.

So encouraged was N. Emopee by this, that his memory even returned, every piece of oboe music ever written, from Bach to Weber, which he had played so often from memory that he'd forgotten it, back on board. He was on a roll.

N. Emopee worried now that he was putting himself at the end of his tether, to where, like an onion peeled layer after layer, there was nothing in the center. He'd just fall apart. As for money, his uncle Rufus had retired completely now. "The heart is willing but the body isn't," he said. As for the tours of the house, these stopped when the bank picked clean the last bone, the final mahogany 2x4, nothing left for anybody to tour. For hope then he had only his arthritic ring fingers, and while they were in the best shape of their lives, stretching, meditating, concentrating, it proved limited to Cleo's linoleum floor. They went right back to their decrepitude when he was somewhere else. It was the same with his improved eyesight, great at the camp, poor again away from it.

That weekend Mr. Snover, the bank manager, came on the property of One Pound Down Street where he intended to secretly pick some pomegranates for his mother-in-law, except that he bumped into N. Emopee instead. "What are you doing down here?" the first words from Snover's pursed lips, for which N. Emopee had no reply, lest he dig himself into an even deeper hole. An hour later, Cleo's camp, the tarpaulin, the Kelvinator refrigerator, the TV, the linoleum floor, everything, was loaded up and heading for the local dump, and by 6:00 that evening, an army of security guards had the place like Fort Knox. This left N. Emopee to fill out a change-of-address form, a change-of-jar form, at the local post office, his new address, Two Pound Down Street down the street, even though there was no such place.

The following morning, in a sleeping bag under a rhododendron bush by the road, at what would be Two Pound Down Street if it existed, he received a letter in his jar asking him to please phone the acquisitions editor at Omni University Press in upstate New York. He had sent them a query letter after reading about them the previous week, raising the whole prospect of university presses for him.

It was regarding his personal narrative *I REFUSE: Memories of a Hayfields and McCays War Resister*, which he'd just completed as an afterthought, a mystery why he hadn't thought of university presses previously. With great anticipation then, he leaped from his bag and hurried down to the Laundromat, to the pay phone at the bottom of the hill, where he searched his pockets in vain for a quarter. This was in the presence of five change machines that had thousands of quarters in them. As luck, good luck, would have it, he found one abandoned on the far counter.

What followed was forty-five minutes, with the charges reversed, during which Ms. Adverse Ponder, the acquisitions editor at Omni, went on with him about how they were developing a new *Peace and Conflict Resolution* series, and how she would very much like to see his book, as he had described it to her in his letter. She said she would be in touch with him when she was ready for him to send it.

Three other small presses, by his mail delivery the next day, expressed an interest in his manuscript, too, wanting to see it right away, to where N. Emopee was beside himself with glee. No sooner did he send out copies to them, though, than all three were returned to him, not to his jar, thank goodness. The editor at Cloud-Hidden Press summed up their view of it this way: "There is nothing new here." The man at Revelations Press, meantime, said to him, "our consortium has not responded." As for the third group, the Out-of-Body Press, they made him an offer, but, "we will publish this only if you are willing to invest in its production and promotion."

N. Emopee, "Invest with what!?"

At the Laundromat at the bottom of the hill, where he had phoned the acquisitions editor at Omni University Press, and where he was now, of all things, doing his laundry, a woman took it upon herself to engage him. "I hear you are a writer," she said to him flat out.

"Pardon me?"

"You see, I'm looking for a 'honey,'" the woman, in all honesty. "I like writers. Would you care to come to my place for a cup of coffee sometime?"

N. Emopee smiled once to be polite.

"I thought you might like to read a novel I purchased this past week. Here it is." She hauled it out of her purse. "Jules at Hick's Used Bookstore said--"

"You know Jules?"

"Everyone knows Jules," she said. "Jules said it is well written, so you should enjoy it, too, I think. We could chat about it then, get to know each other. What do you say?"

N. Emopee didn't know what to make of this, even as he glanced down to see a well-worn copy of *A Single Man* by Christopher Isherwood. Reluctant to be entirely rude, he accepted the offered novel, a brief nod from him the indication that he would have a look at it. As a single man himself he would find something in it to like, he guessed. As for going to this lady's place to discuss it, not on his life.

It so happened *A Single Man* was about a college teacher in Los Angeles, a "Roads Scholar" as he called himself, someone who drove from one lecture to another, thirty miles apart sometimes, piecing together enough to make a living. George, the central character, was a writer too, just like N. Emopee, but who had, unlike N. Emopee, a small private income from his published work. This, coupled with the little that teaching paid him, kept him in reasonable stead.

Reading on, he discovered that George was a homosexual, to the extent in fact that all the remainder of the book was about it. This caused N. Emopee to realize, could it be more obvious, that this was why the woman loaned the novel to him. She wanted to see whether he was that way, too, which would be evident, she believed, by his response to it. If he said to her, "I liked the book, but didn't like that the main character is homosexual," it would be a green light for her to continue her pursuit of him. If, on the other hand, he stated that he liked the book and especially liked that the central character was homosexual, she would waste no more time on him.

When he saw her at the Laundromat two days later, he handed the novel back to her. "Thanks for lending this to me." Seeing that this was all she was going to get from him, she walked now to the man at the dryer-sheet dispenser, a quick breath before, "I hear you are a writer."

As it turned out he had another thing in common with this Christopher Isherwood. The biographical sketch on the back of *A Single Man* revealed that he was a devotee of eastern religions, Vedanta in his case. Moreover, Alan Watts, N. Emopee's radio philosopher, listed Isherwood in that group of World War II immigrants to America whom he called the British Mystical Expatriates, to include Isherwood, Aldous Huxley, Gerald Heard, and Felix Greene.

And with this, as he read still more about Isherwood, came the whole bunch, Sri Ramakrishna, Swami

Vivekananda, Swami Brahmananda, Swami Prabhavananda, J. Krishnamurti, theosophists Besant, Olcott, Judge, Leadbeater, to join the others he knew about already, Buddhist scholar-devotees Evans-Wentz and David-Neel, and Madame Blavatsky, individuals he subsequently referred to as his "spiritual family." The woman at the Laundromat had shown him his family. Well, she didn't show him, but something did.

Ms. Ponder, the acquisitions editor at Omni University Press announced in a new letter to him that she was ready now to see his personal narrative. Yet, one week after he mailed it to her, she sent him a rejection letter. In a handwritten note at the end, though, she said, "I have included here the reports of the two outside readers, specialists in antiwar literature, upon which this rejection is based. The reports contain suggestions on ways you can improve the work, which, if you cared to implement them, might warrant another look by us. But I can't guarantee anything."

He would make the changes immediately, of course.

Which was when he bumped into Professor Bob down in town, who told him about an available teaching position in the Oboe department at West Virginia Academy up at Sheet Lake where he taught, a sabbatical replacement he said, a golden opportunity for him if he was at all interested, which, naturally, he wasn't. Still, in memory of his Eunice, who liked teachers, and of Rem who taught at Sourbrook Community College for a time, and of his adopted sister

April, a biology teacher, and then because of some vague feeling of his, a sense of unfinished business, he phoned the chairman for an interview.

The next afternoon, his curriculum vita in hand, he twitched before the department's two senior faculty, the chairman and his first lieutenant, both oboists, with whom he had an instant rapport. Indeed not twenty minutes into their exchange the chairman ask him flat out, "How interested <u>are</u> you, Mr. Emopee?"

N. Emopee did not hesitate. "<u>Very</u> interested," with a wave.

Except that he was not interested, not as much as he wanted to be, or as much as he felt he should be, or that he might come to be should he give it a good try this time, were he inclined to do so. He was not so disposed, never was, and never would be, so much as he was only being desperate. And with this, teaching was never again an option for him.

The lady at the Laundromat mentioning Jules the last week reminded N. Emopee that it had been ages since he had set foot in Hick's Used Bookstore--were the books used or was it the store that was used? Thus, he marched back down High Street to the familiar beep and bark at Hick's front door.

Once inside, however, he discovered that all hands, Mr. Hick, Jules, and Raymond, were packing book boxes. For Mr. Hick the previous night's earthquake--although N. Emopee had not felt it--was the last straw. He couldn't take it any longer, so lock, stock, and Bert, he was moving to Florida, where all there was were hurricanes.

An earthquake the previous night? It seemed Raymond had taken Mr. Hick to see the movie *Earthquake* at the theatre next door, which had something to do with it most likely.

A long yellow moving van ground to a stop at the front door and an equally long line of dollies began their loading of the boxed books.

"Morganhill won't be the same without you," N. Emopee admitted to Mr. Hick. It was a sentiment having more truth to it than it at first sounded, for all three buildings there, Hick's, the Warner theatre next door, and the Bang building next door on the other side, where Emily's Typical Typing Service once pecked, were now condemned and set to be demolished the first thing in the morning. The city building inspector had seen the earthquake movie himself last night.

All of N. Emopee's efforts were focused now on his revising his personal narrative manuscript along the lines suggested by the two outside readers for the Omni University Press. The one reader especially, who remained anonymous, of course, but who had a special interest in seeing the book improved, apparently, a fellow anti-warrior possibly, he particularly wanted to please. At the same time, N. Emopee thought about what he would do if the work was turned down yet another time, one last time, was rejected by the *Peace and Conflict Resolution* series editor, the ultimate judge, according to Ms. Ponder. A painful thought, absolutely. Not helping, a new owner of his hill, yes a new owner had emerged, one D. J. Fearce of Fearce Development, who had managed to level the entire top of the hill, when no one was looking, so that N. Emopee had nowhere to live at all now, not even under that rhododendron bush he called Two Pound Down Street. All he had was his old blimp-of- a-station wagon, which, regrettably, was, at the moment, filled with so much junk, necessary junk, that there was no room for himself in it.

A home altar symbolized a person's Buddha nature, the sitting place of the Buddha within himself, which for N. Emopee had been a wooden oriental cabinet. It was his grandmother's liquor cabinet at one time, funnily a booze cabinet, but in which he currently had housed another kind of intoxication, his library of eastern philosophy. A plaster-cast Buddha a foot high in a lotus pose resided in the cabinet in the beginning, soon after he first purchased it years ago, and before his exile to Erie.

This Buddha he bought in Mexico the one time he was out on the west coast, even as he wondered if there was such a thing as Mexicans who were Buddhists. Mexican Buddhists he'd never heard of, not that there couldn't be. Rows of the Buddhas, along with pink flamingos and spitting frogs, where the vendors had them set out along the road in Tijuana, made him doubt it. The Buddha he purchased, however, he took a liking to the moment he saw it, so much so that it accompanied him everywhere he went, even into exile, the Buddha in exile.

Yet, after Erie, when he returned to Morganhill, he left behind his cast Buddha. He left it in a storage locker in his apartment building for whoever might find it, his having concluded that such images were the stuff of popularized religion. It was not what Buddhism was about, he felt, even as now he missed the guy.

Or was it the Buddha's message he missed? "Work out your own salvation with diligence," as Ed his former painter used to quote, which meant that one must pay attention to maya, or illusion, not an easy thing for anyone, much less for N. Emopee to do, as he was particularly prone to illusion. A fish, for example, did not know it was in the water because it was never out of it, and so it was with humans. Humans have never lived in any other state than what Alan Watts termed the great sleep walk. Seeing anything other than the illusion was hard.

The plaster-cast Buddha gone, his oriental cabinet became the home of his favorite books on eastern philosophy. Every time he opened its double doors, a hand-painted chinoiserie mural on each panel, a gust of sandalwood, "the smell of Buddhism," wafted out over him. He had sandalwood joss sticks stored in the long drawer below the double doors, explaining why the scent was so prevalent. His eager eyes would grasp the line of titles then, from Asoka to Ramakrishna, didn't he feel their energy, the charged presence all those wise souls, as though they were standing there looking back at him.

Just then a startling notion entered his mind. Concerning his personal narrative he wondered whether its central issue, his resistance to the Hayfields and McCays war, wasn't the high point of his life, the apex of his existence, to where that was the reason for his being. It left all of his other doings, his oboing, his story analyzing, his screenwriting, his fiction and nonfiction writing, even his hoped-for refuge, somewhere in the dust.

Guided by the outside readers' reports, N. Emopee completed first one, then a second full revision of *I REFUSE*, supported by Ms. Ponder, who continued to encourage him, while at the same time warning him of a possible second and final rejection. Still, he was feeling good about it all, and about himself, confident that despite how things looked for him at the moment, he was on the right track. Indeed, he was on the only track he could be on, he felt, his destiny awaiting him, if it wasn't already upon him.

At long last came the decision from Omni University Press, the conclusion finally to the carrot on the stick for months now. As a smoke screen, a way of preparing himself for bad news, if that should be it, he took the attitude that, while he created this new book of his, he did not do so as N. Emopee the writer but as N. Emopee a nobody, who coincidentally wrote books, how eccentric of him. Yet, in the end, this neat maneuver did him little good, for the Omni

University Press, the *Peace and Conflict Resolution* series editor specifically, a Mr. Shoop, did indeed reject the work, concluding simply, "it's not right for us."

In their subsequent damage control modes, N. Emopee and Ms. Ponder scrambled to see if there wasn't a negotiable adjustment to the book, something that would return it to consideration. An outside copy editor could be contracted to polish problematic syntax, for example. One of the criticisms was that it did not sound sufficiently like it was from an academic press.

"*I REFUSE* is not a text book," N. Emopee, bitterly, in response. Frustrated, fed up, frantic, he went on to nix the outside copy editor idea even, with the result that the manuscript was returned to him promptly the next day. A letter from Ms. Ponder wished him luck in finding another publisher, his one ally at Omni out now, too.

Chapter Fourteen
The Unexpected

Regretting his irritation, N. Emopee phoned Ms. Ponder right away the following morning, only to find that she would not take or return his call. When, at the end of the day, he, by a fluke, did get her on the line, she did all the talking. She chastised him for undercutting her negotiations with the series editor, reminding him that his personal narrative was not, after all, *THE ILIAD*, not a masterpiece, and that if he had hopes of ever having anything published in the future, he'd better learn what the word flexibility meant.

"Whatever you say," N. Emopee at the end of it with a whisper. "Whatever you want. If only you could know what I've put into it."

"You and every other writer, Mr. N. Emopee, you and the rest of the writing world and their books. But if you want I will try it one last time."

"I'll be here." At the Laundromat.

At two o'clock that afternoon, she rang him back. "It's no use."

In *I REFUSE*, N. Emopee recounted how the Hayfields and McCays war was unexpected. The two families, first of all, had staked out their territories clearly. The Hayfields were exclusively in the northern half of the state, the McCays in the southern, divided by the 38th parallel down in the town of Sutton, the geographical center of the state. This created a North West Virginia and a South West Virginia.

If the Hayfields had an advantage, it was because, unbeknownst to everyone except their inner circle, they had military advisors assisting them, officers of the North Vietnamese army. They had been successful in their own country in the late '60's, so they believed they could help out here. Among their accomplishments to date, a network of underground tunnels between north and south, and a Ho Chi Minh Trail, dubbed the Homer C. Moon Trail, after the farmer on whose land the trail began. It was for transporting equipment and supplies through the backwoods.

Also to the Hayfield's advantage, a pro-war governor in Arnie Hackett, who came to power when the anti-war governor Zelda Dilworth was mysteriously found in a coma. "Let the war begin!" Hackett's proclamation, euphorically his declaration the moment he learned that war was at hand. "Long live Wally Baron!" a cold Papst chasing Hackett's gulp of Old Crow at his desk at eight o'clock in the morning. Baron was the worst crook in the state's history.

Now, the objective of the Hayfields was certain enough, to end their feud with the McCays once and for all, in their favor of course, the same as the McCays' only in reverse. This left the question, what was in it for the North Vietnamese?

N. Emopee had not yet met Professor Bob, but it turned out that he was researching the matter for his new course, *Who are the North Vietnamese?* The professor concluded that it was casualties. They had not yet gotten over their huge death toll in the Vietnamese war, three times that of the Americans. This chance to even the numbers was too tempting for them. "It is the way wars are perpetuated," explained Bob. It didn't hurt that the Hayfields were paying them a lot of money.

Room Six at the Motel Six at the Arter D. Cepov Bridge connecting Morganhill with Westhill, was N. Emopee's temporary residence, thanks to the motel's owner, who, like him, was also an anti-warrior. N. Emopee liked Room Six because it had a view, even if it was only of the Missing River. The reason he was there was because Rem was removing all the water-damaged wallpaper in their house, legions of contractors everywhere.

Another anti-warrior was a signwriter named Dar Handog, an eighty-year-old Swede still at it after all these years, out of the Blind Stone Print Shop over on Walnut Street. Dar made up fifty signs for him to nail up around the city, signs that proclaimed "NO TO WAR."

Unlike before, though, this time Dar inscribed each sign with the image of an oboe down in the lower right-hand corner, as if anyone in town wouldn't know already who was leading this protest. These signs, these placards of N. Emopee's, were, after all, a call to arms. They were a call to dissent, which he hoped would bring people out into the streets by the thousands.

Was it these posters, up for a mere 24 hours before the warmongers torn them down again, the reason for the letter in his motel mailbox two days later. "Greetings," the letter read. In his motel bathrobe, the Missing River yawning vacantly over his hunched right shoulder, he read that the Hayfields/North Vietnamese had just instituted a draft, and that the first to be called up were thirty-four year old Third-Chair oboists who, accordingly, were to report for service the next morning. It gave the address where they were to appear, where he was to appear.

So outraged was N. Emopee by this that he had a mind to join the McCays down south just for spite, except that they were drafting him, too; his motel mailbox contained a letter from them as well. And they had Vietnamese on their side now, too, if their draft notice was to be believed. On board was former air force commander and vice president of South Vietnam, along with ten of his top generals, living these days in Clarksburg, West Virginia, where they owned liquor stores. Their formidability as a weapon was doubtful anymore, however. What were they going to do, toss bottles of Jack Daniels at the other side?

"I have my rights!" N. Emopee could only shriek, half-shriek, well aware that few rights of any kind remained in the state, due to the war. Even so, he wasted no time in applying for conscientious objector status, sending both the Hayfields and McCays all the forms, along with a copy of his membership in the American Buddhist Society, sure to strike a chord with the Vietnamese, even though they were all Lutherans now.

That not a single soul turned out for his first protest rally at the Courthouse Square on High Street later that day was an indication to him how all this was going to go. This was nothing like the throngs he expected. What he did not anticipate was the popularity of the war, how everyone had become bored with peace over the years, and here was something to get their attention again. N. Emopee, it seemed, was the only one resisting.

And it appeared now that he and Rem would never get back One Pound Down Street, the hill annexed overnight by the Hayfields.

When, at the prescribed time and place, 8:00 a.m. at the McDonald's restaurant on Willey Street, he failed to turn up for his induction into either the Hayfields' or the McCays' armies, if they could be called armies, more like posses, they came looking for him. Never mind that they left behind the fifteen other thirty-four year old Third-Chair oboists who did show up. Because N. Emopee was the one they really wanted. N. Emopee was the troublemaker. And so, just as he was turning on *The Today Show* on his television at the motel, there came a thumping at his door. Thinking it the maid come to make up his room already, he flung open the door.

At his doorstep, his worse nightmare.

"Hi, 'Shit.' Hey, Clay," the best he could manage. For here were the two patriarchs, Ol' Man "Shit" Hayfield and C. M. McCay, Clay Mudd McCay. Six-foot-three and skinny as a rail, the former wore a scraggly gray beard, badly in need of vacuuming, his skin ruddy with psoriasis. His coveralls were streaked with blood.

No less so, the shirt and pants of Clay McCay, albeit not as filthy somehow, probably because he was younger than "Shit," more vain. And Clay had no beard, just a long mustache grown back into his sideburns, gray, though, too. All the while Clay rotated his tongue in his mouth, menacingly rolled it in his cheeks, as if he'd just eaten a baby.

The only other time N. Emopee was face to face with any Hayfield or McCay was when he was kidnapped by "Shit's" and Clay's four eldest sons, who bound and gagged him and put him on a plane for Erie P.A., location of his exile.

The glare in the old men's eyes on this day, however, made it clear that they intended no such civility. N. Emopee was on "Shit's" shit list, and would be on Clay's, too, if he could write.

"Can I offer you gents a Coke? How about a nice mug of blood," on deaf ears, for in the next instant they pulled out their revolvers and fired at him.

Stunned, N. Emopee doubled over, dropped to his knees, then crumpled into a heap in the doorway.

This Ol' Man "Shit" Hayfield and Clay Mudd McCay were direct descendants of Thomas Henderson "Demon" Hayfield and Raymond "Lil' Ray" McCay who lived in the mid-1800's, according to the local Mormon, the state Mormon. He had conducted a genealogy study for governor Hackett to promote the souvenir plastic plates he would be selling during the war, dishes with "Demon" and "Lil' Ray" in the center of them, and then the generations of other Hayfields and McCays all around the edges, "Shit" and Clay included.

If this researching Mormon chose to remain nameless, it was so he wouldn't suffer reprisals from the two families for what he discovered about them. He learned, for one, that it was a myth that the Hayfields married into the McCays family and vice versa over the years, the Hayfields and McCays not the Montagues and Capulets, no Romeos and Juliets here. Quite the contrary. The marrying took place within their own families, much like early Royals attempted in Europe, to keep the line clean, and with the same disastrous results. It explained why, for instance, "Shit" had six fingers on his right hand, two of which, the thumb and forefinger, were webbed, and why Clay had only one eye, in the middle of his forehead.

The feud began in 1864 when "Lil' Ray" happened onto the property of his neighbor Flint Hayfield where he was startled to find one of his hogs in Flint's pen, a clear case, and a major no-no, of hog rustling. The accusation brought "Demon" out of the woodwork and the fight was on. These were the days when the two families lived on either side of the Tow River, the Hayfields in southern West Virginia and the McCays in northern Kentucky. Now that they had proliferated and taken up sole residence in West Virginia, the generations of hard feelings were at their peak.

Following the volley from the revolvers of "Shit" and Clay, N. Emopee remained in a pile in the doorway of Room Six at the Motel Six down by the Arter D. Cepov Bridge, where at last the maid turned up to make up his room except that she screamed instead. Dashing to him, she held her ear to his mouth to see if he was breathing, fumbling in her apron, at the same time, for the pamphlet she'd been given the day before during her Motel Six maid-orientation class for new employees, on what to do if a patron got shot in a doorway.

"Mr. Centipede, Mr. Centipede," in her broken English, but to no avail, until at last, his left eye squinting open, N. Emopee whispered to her, "Are they gone?"

"Are who gone, Mr. Centipede?" the maid, out of breath now from hyperventilating.

"Good," N. Emopee. He pulled himself back to his feet with a single jerk.

"What happened to you? Are you all right?"

"Not to worry. I wear bullet proof pajamas."

The decision facing him now, he wrote in *I REFUSE*, was whether to stay and fight to end the war or whether to yield to the majority who seemed glad the war was on again. Except that they were not glad. This was the key to it. Like the Europeans in World War I who willingly ran off to the front for the sheer adventure of it, the novelty here was wearing off just as quickly.

The people seemed more resigned this time, however. The war was the war. It would run its course, they hoped, until eventually it petered out, except that the embers, they didn't realize, would remain, only to be fanned back to life in a few more years.

Meantime, it was clear to everyone that it made no difference whether the patriarchs, "Shit" and Clay, were still around or not. They could kill each other off this very day, or have each other killed off, were it not for their becoming friends of sorts, allies in a way, under certain circumstances, as when they turned up together at N. Emopee's doorstep at the Motel Six.

It had his name on it, sure enough, so it wasn't an ad, or wasn't just any ad. The return address of P.O. Box 333, New Martinsville, West Virginia, though, did not ring a bell to him to him. A miracle it was, anyway, that he received it,

on the move now as he was, in the underground, a marked
man. This was to say that the last thing he needed now was
for the Motel Six to leave the light on for him. His thumb
through the seal, he folded the letter open.

*Dear N. Emopee: The Hayfields and McCays are
Yin and Yang, mutually arising opposites, where the
one does not, cannot exist without the other.*

It was from Ed, N. Emopee's new acquaintance from the
Buddhist monastery on the Ohio River.

*The Hayfields are gregarious and outgoing,
optimistic, the sunny side of the mountain, while the
McCays are melancholy and introverted, pessimistic,
the side of the mountain in the shade. Their hatred
for each other is what they have in common.*

*The war between them will end not when one family
defeats the other--this will not happen because
there are too many of them and they are too
evenly matched--but when they are both defeated
together by something more powerful than they are
themselves, by a common enemy. Complicating it
is that the North Vietnamese in Morganhill, and the
South Vietnamese in Beckley, hate each other too.*

*It may be that there is nothing to be done, wu wei, no-
action, in Taoism, letting things resolve themselves*

in a natural and spontaneous way, the answer. All things in their time.

It is an appealing thought were it not for the drafts the Hayfields and McCays have instituted, and with which you, I understand, are all too familiar, under the penalty of death. Six anti-draft militant Third-Chair oboists, your fellow Third-Chair oboists, throwing buckets of blood at the Hayfields and McCays down in Sutton, the front, is to their endless credit. But it cost them their lives. Both sides shot them on the spot. No, the draft provides a steady flow of manpower to them and with enough propaganda on both sides to make the war seem justified, this thing could go on for a decade.

Yours,
Ed.

The war would end when both families were defeated by something more powerful than themselves, did he say? Militant oboists, did he say? Why didn't he think of it before?

At the library the next morning N. Emopee emailed the president of the American Oboe Association, Fred Baronette, about this, only to receive a reply right away from his secretary that he was no longer the president. Indeed, the association was just concluding their secret conclave there in Chicago, selecting as their next "oboe pope," one

Hieronymus Hup. "You've heard of him have you?" she wrote.

"Hieronymus Hup of the Stiff Arm Symphony in Morganhill, West Virginia?" he emailed back. "He is my conductor."

So, old Hup was president of the AOA now was he? Hup lived there in West Virginia, so he was already sympathetic to the cause.

"Well, Heirrrrr Emopee," said Hup, picking up the receiver of the phone. N. Emopee called the number the secretary gave him. Hup's installment, it turned out, was taking place right there at that moment in his predecessor's, Baronette's office. "What can I do for you?"

N. Emopee got right to it, explaining all about his plan to overwhelm the warring parties, the Hayfields and McCays and the rest of them, with the worst nightmare of their lives, oboe music. In this way he could bring an end to the war before it was too late, before it was out of control.

"But why? Why do you carrrre? Nobody else carrrres," Hup.

"You know better than that, surely. People are waiting for someone to step forward, somebody to lead the way to peace."

"Someone like you?"

"Someone like you, Mr. Hup. You have the power now. Issue a 'call to oboes' to the membership, 'calling all oboes.'"

Two days later, West Virginia was crawling with oboists. Hup had acquiesced. In small bands, literally small bands, complete with conductors, they positioned themselves as not to get shot at but still within hearing range of the enemies. All the while, they carried flags representing the states they were from, some from as far away as Hawaii.

By the end of the week, N. Emopee, representing the Oboe Coalition, as they called themselves, sat at a large table in a tent in Sutton, the front. A peace conference was underway. There was objection to the shape of the table, a five-sided affair representing the five factions, the Hayfields, the North Vietnamese, the McCays, the South Vietnamese, and the Oboists, all of them avoiding the fifth side of the table because that was the one facing Pittsburgh, considered bad luck. The Oboists further rejected the shape because it looked too much like the Pentagon, and they didn't want to bring the U.S. government into it. Thus, the five-sided table was replaced by a round one, and, for added measure, they all changed chairs every hour.

It didn't help that "Shit" Hayfield and Clay McCay kept dozing off, and that the North Vietnamese ate Chinese takeout the whole time and the South Vietnamese, Thai takeout, which, with such a mess, didn't make for much accord. Despite this, the positions of the Hayfields and McCays were clear from the outset. Stop the music.

A slam dunk, though, the peace was not. Enormous egos all around had to be appeased, promises of book deals, towns named after them, the Nobel Peace Prize. The worst of the lot were the Oboists, including Hup. Hup didn't do anything, beyond issuing that memo to the membership, that "call to oboes," and he was reluctant even to do this, but now he wanted a statue of himself in the state capital.

All of this, and more, was in N. Emopee's book.

"Hell is getting what you want," N. Emopee, to himself, as he sat scrunched on a plush sofa in the spacious faculty residence of Professor Wishborn "Bob" Corbette. Faculty and students were gathered there for a formal dinner and discussion of his just published personal narrative. After taking it to another publisher, War's End Press, which specialized in just his kind of resistance, N. Emopee got in print after all, and as these things sometimes went, he did much better by them, not only a soft cover but a hard cover as well.

Thor Snover, the bank manager, and N. Emopee agreed to meet up at One Pound Down Street, which wasn't there anymore. There they stood at high noon, on top of the hill completely graded now, the house but a memory, the pomegranate grove out without a trace, too, even the great fence surrounding the property now history.

There they swayed, just the two of them, the sun a smudge in the hazy August sky, the wind rustling every so often, just enough to shoo away the mosquitoes. The humidity, meantime, was, as always at this time of year, enough to cut with a knife. Pulling a handkerchief from his back pocket, Snover swabbed the sweat from his brow.

"Fearce Development is no longer interested in the project, you may as well know. West Virginia is too unstable for them, they said, what with the constant threat of war. They thought they could handle it, but they can't. They've moved on to Maryland. The land is the bank's again."

"Oh?"

"Do you want it back? For that refuge of yours I mean."

"The remnants of foreign wars would have liked it."

Snover, walking now, N. Emopee in his wake, only to stop dead center in the property, as if in a bull's eye. "How about you buy back the whole place, land and everything? I'll make you an offer you can't refuse."

N. Emopee looked over.

"The fact is, Emopee, I haven't been able to get anyone seriously to take this property from the very beginning, and I've been trying everyday since we took possession of it last summer. Fearce came the closest."

N. Emopee stared.

Snover, turning to face him, "We can write it up this afternoon."

"Nobody wanted this land either when Rem bought it seventy years ago. It's come full circle. As for the remnants of foreign wars refuge, I am stepping away from it. Rem made me swear that I would see it through to completion, but the statute of limitations on it has passed. It was to be a monumental project to begin with, but it is impossible now. I would have to start all over. There is nothing here now but what could have been."

"I'm sorry," Snover.

"The Tao is having its way." This was Ed, at what was to be the dedication of the new refuge.

"<u>Something</u> is having its way," N. Emopee.

N. Emopee did not pray as a rule, despite feeling spirituality in his heart. Yet, on this occasion he could not avoid it. The first words from his lips, however, or rather the first words he was about to say, raised the hair on the back of his neck. It was as though he'd stepped off a cliff. He gasped loudly and nearly fainted. A channel had opened in him, and it scared him half to death.

THE END

About the Author

Donald Laird Simons was born September 29, 1945 in Morgantown, West Virginia. He graduated from West Virginia University in 1967 with a BA in Psychology and in 1970 with an MA in Drama. In 1981, Mr. Simons earned a Doctorate in Communication-Drama from the University of Southern California.

In 1992, his personal narrative, *I REFUSE: Memories of a Vietnam War Objector*, was published by The Broken Rifle Press, Trenton, New Jersey.

He is the author of a large blog, *Donald L. Simons on Vedanta, Buddhism*, at donaldsimons.blogspot.com.

Currently, Mr. Simons lives in Costa Mesa, California.